Emily Thornton Charles

**Hawthorn Blossoms**

Emily Thornton Charles

**Hawthorn Blossoms**

ISBN/EAN: 9783337279257

Printed in Europe, USA, Canada, Australia, Japan

Cover: Foto ©Andreas Hilbeck / pixelio.de

More available books at **www.hansebooks.com**

# HAWTHORN BLOSSOMS.

BY

## EMILY THORNTON CHARLES.

(EMILY HAWTHORNE.)

---

" They learn in suffering
What they teach in song."

SHELLEY.

---

PHILADELPHIA:
J. B. LIPPINCOTT & CO.
1876.

# DEDICATION.

---

# EXPLANATORY.

---

If, in giving expression to the thoughts that throng my mind and the emotions that swell within my heart, I shall touch a vibrating chord of sympathy that thrills the bosom of another, and gives expression to another's joy or sorrow, which is as giving voice to those who were dumb, and as bringing the relief that is brought by tears to the too full heart, then this little volume shall have fulfilled its mission.

THE AUTHOR.

# CONTENTS.

# CONTENTS.

# PROLOGUE.

WHY, when I seek to float on wings of fancy
To realms of imagery, and rest me in my high-flown
    course
Upon the mountain-tops of Reverie; or, soaring up-
    ward,
Reach the highest pinnacle of thought—
Why is it that, when thus I long to fly,
My wings are feeble, and refuse to bear me up?
And something, what 'tis I know not, drags me down,
And will not let me rise; and I must needs
Grow timid—scarce will try the flight nor use
The pinions wherewith Nature hath provided me?
  What, then, wouldst have me do—what course
    pursue?
Must I, then, train these wings of thought, and
Strengthen them, that they may bear me ever up
And bravely onward; or clip them close, and ever be
    content,
Like barnyard fowl, or eaglet of its pinions shorn,
To hover near the ground?

May I not bathe these wings, to start their growth,
In limpid streams of Poesy—nor yet approach those
    famous rivers,
Rhyme and Reason—nor tempt my timid muse
To sound their praises?

INDIANAPOLIS, September 1, 1875.

# TO MY FRIENDS.

A SPRAY of flowers I bring thee, friendship's token;
  Hoping, though many wither 'neath the noontide
    sun,
Bedewed with tears from clouds of grief unspoken,
  In memory's vase will live and linger one.

My path was rough, few flowers grew by the way,
  But finding on a jagged, rocky slope,
There gathered I this simple hawthorn spray;
  And now bring I to thee a flower that breathes of
    hope.

Behold, the morn beyond the night is breaking
  That bringeth forth a brighter, fairer day;
And o'er the earth the glorious sun, awaking,
  Riseth, and sends the sunbeams out to play.

Thus glorious hope doth rise within the bosom,
  Beyond the gloomy night of grief and care;
So may these flowers mature in perfect blossom,
  Bright hopes spring up, choking the weed despair.

Hope's buds are sometimes but the opening flowers,
   That, ere they blossom, crushed and blasted lie;
So buds of thought, beguiling weary hours,
   May die, and yet their mission ne'er can die.

What though on earth our hopes ne'er find fruition,
   And blossoms fade and reach a sere decay;
These flowers have still fulfilled their truest mission,
   And sometimes driven doubt and fear away.

And, though my garland has no beauteous blossom,
   No budding thought that sprang to perfect bloom,
Bury it with me, folded on my bosom;
   My flowers of hope will live beyond the tomb.

Receive my flowers; they have no shine of splendor,
   Yet costlier tribute ne'er was brought to king;
Their price was love, grief, pain; and oh! remember,
   The gift, though small, was all I had to bring.

# MY LITTLE SISTER MINA.

A school "composition," written when the author was thirteen
years of age.)

I HAVE a little sister dear,
  Just three years old to-day ;
I've watched her growth from year to year
  With a sister's love, they say.

I think she's very handsome,
  Though others may not see
In her those charms so winsome,
  Which are so dear to me.

Her golden locks in ringlets hang
  From morning until night ;
Oh, sure the poets never sang
  Of fairer, prettier sight.

Her cheeks are like the rose—so red ;
  Her eyes, the violet's hue ;
A dimpled chin, a golden head,
  A laugh that thrills you through.

Her skin like alabaster fair ;
  Lips rose-leaves dipped in dew,
And written on them plainly there
  Is, " I've a kiss for you."

January, 1854.

# DEVOTED TO YOU.

'Tis sad to starve a heart, love,
  So worshipful and true;
'Tis wrong to doubt a soul, love,
  That's centred but in you.

But if you doubt me still, love,
  Then let me tell you true;
The heart you will not prize, love,
  For aye will turn to you.

Then cast away all fear, love;
  Believe me fond and true;
This heart which throbs for you, love,
  No other love e'er knew.

Then let the years pass by, love,
  Come joy, and sorrow, too,
This heart you'll ever find, love,
  Devoted but to you.

July, 1872.

# SERENADE.

I'm listening beneath your window
  For the sound of your winning voice;
And the tread of your hastening footsteps
  My heart maketh gladly rejoice.

Come, love, and give me the greeting
  That 'tis only your lips can give;
I will cherish it ever so fondly,
  So long as we both, dear, shall live.

Love-light in your eye beams brightly;
  I'm sure it is beaming for me.
Let it ever be thus, oh, my darling!
  And happy, how happy I'll be!

We'll journey along together,
  As happy as happy can be;
We'll recall when we met 'neath the window
  And you gave a greeting to me.

The trials of life are coming—
  I'll meet them with never a sigh,
While I have but your sweet voice to cheer me,
  And the light of your loving eye.

July, 1872.

2*

# THE LIFE-BOAT.

WE'RE afloat, we're afloat,
And our bark of life is a leaky boat.
Sometimes we rest
On a tidal crest,
Or again we sink
O'er the watery brink.
Sometimes on the summit of waves we ride,
Like a child at rest
On its mother's breast,
Then down we sink with the billowy tide.

So, up and down
In this world are we thrown:
Now, beaten and drenched by the waves of scorn;
Then, on billows of hope,
With life's breakers we cope,
But we sink in despair ere we reach the bourn,

So buffeted we
By the pitiless sea,
And the storm and the tempest carry us fast.
Our bark is frail—
Can ill stand the gale—
But we'll hope we shall safely reach harbor at last.

Now hidden are we
In the trough of the sea ;
But again we rise as the waves sweep past.
Our troubles soon o'er
We will struggle no more,
But be moored in the shelter of heaven at last.

August, 1872.

---

## HOW I "FELL INTO LOVE."

NEAR the river of love
I stood, on the brink ;
That I might stumble in,
Why did I not think ?

A fair maiden passed by,
And I started to run ;
But a glance from her eye,
And the mischief was done.

Sunshine in her hair
Surely dazzled my eye,
For I fell in the stream
As my heart heaved a sigh.

With the current of love
    I am struggling away;
But so feeble am I
    In the current I stay.

In the vortex of love
    I am whirling around;
If she saves me not soon,
    I shall surely be drowned.

Come, then, quickly to me,
    Oh maiden, so fair!
Or soon I shall sink
    In the gulf of despair.

August, 1872.

## TOO LATE.

I once decided not to love—
No such power should my heart move :
I would be, unlike the rest,
Heart-free, for I deemed it best.

And so I would not let Love in
To my heart —'twould be a sin :

So I dreamt, and so I thought
'Twould be wise to lock Love out.

But I locked the door too late
Of my heart; my very fate
Was enthralled by your power,
Ere I thought to lock the door.

August, 1872.

## A FRAGMENT.

To be, to do, and to suffer—
These words do tell
(I have conned them well)
Our lot on earth.

I live, I exist;
Of the work to be done
I do what I can,
And believe me, dear friend,
          I suffer.

May, 1873.

# CLOUD-LAND.

THE clouds, the beautiful clouds!
　　Oh, could I but write,
　　As I see them to-night!
The beautiful, varying clouds.

The clouds, ever-changing clouds,
　　Floating airily by,
　　Weaving webs in the sky,
The beautiful, silvery clouds.

The clouds, the mountainous clouds,
　　Are uplifted so high
　　In the blue of the sky—
The towering mountains of clouds.

The clouds, the luminous clouds,
　　And clouds like lace,
　　Nearly veiling the face
Of the luminous, sunset clouds.

The clouds, most glorious clouds,
　　Rising higher and higher—
　　Great pillars of fire—
The grandest of glorious clouds.

The clouds, the terrible clouds!
    They gather and roll,
    Like despair o'er the soul—
Most terrible, threatening clouds!

The clouds, the storm-laden clouds,
    They with tear-drops of rain
    Moisten earth's face again,
The clouds, heavy rain-laden clouds.

The clouds, summer, sunset clouds,
    They are, after the rain,
    Golden burnished again,
By the sun peeping under the clouds.

The beautiful, beautiful clouds!
    Oh, could I but write,
    As I sit here to-night,
All the grandeur, the beauty of clouds!

July, 1872.

# THE SWEET SAD THOUGHT.

THE saddest yet sweetest thoughts of all—
Fruition gone beyond recall—
Are thoughts unuttered by tongue or pen ;
The memories of what might have been.

What might have been may never be.
In thine own heart's depth look and see,
As many another one hath seen,
Sweet sorrow for what might have been.

Why sweet, if sad and past recall ?
Love lost were better than none at all,
It casts o'er the heart, like silvery sheen,
Sweet, sad thoughts of what might have been.

Love lives in memories of the past.
In dreams these memories thick and fast
Come thronging.   Bliss in dreams ! ah, then,
There are visions of Heaven in what might have been.

# A  FAREWELL  TO  SIGHT.

"A lady near Covington, Kentucky, whose sight was failing, upon consulting a physician was told that in a few hours she would be totally blind. She went home, took a farewell look at familiar objects, and had her two little children dressed in their prettiest attire and brought before her, that as the light faded from her eyes their latest sight should rest on them."

DEAR Lord, and must it, can it be
That I no more again shall see?
    No more forever—
The earth's soft carpet, brightly green,
Or watch the wavering, shimmering sheen
    Play o'er the river?

No more the fragrant spring-time flowers
That erstwhile gave me many hours
    Of sweet delight—
Nor mossy banks 'neath shady trees
With leaflets swaying in the breeze
    Shall glad my sight.

No more my upward gaze shall rest
Upon the towering mountain's crest
    Grand and sublime—

Nor watch the singing, rippling rill
Flow swiftly 'neath the rocky hill
　　Ceaseless as time.

I'll see no mor   the waving grain,
Nor vessels riding o'er the main
　　Of broad expanse.
No more these longing eyes shall look
On scenes of life from nature's book—
　　Not e'en a glance.

No more the cattle o'er the dale,
Nor cot half hidden in the vale,
　　The scene (for me) enhance.
Or sight of glorious works of art,
Or nature's pictures fill my heart,
　　My soul entrance.

No more I'll see the sun uprise,
Nor e'er again, with beaming eyes,
　　Meet his bright beams—
For as he slowly sinks from sight
My sight goes also ; I, ere night,
　　See but in dreams.

Bring now my precious treasures here,
My darling babes, so fair, so dear,
　　Their childish grace—

That I may linger fondly o'er
Each lineament; in my mind may store
    Each pictured face.

Robed in pure vestage fair and white,
Thus let them fade from loving sight
    Like sun at even—
My heart shall watch them day by day
Tho' eyes see not—them I will pray
    To see in heaven.

---

## A MOTHER'S ANGUISH.

### THE DREAM.

    OH, Myla, my darling,
    My sunbeam, my starling,
My birdling has flitted, my darling is gone.
    Oh, why didst thou leave me?
    Or why shouldst thou grieve me?
My darling, my precious, why leave me alone?

    She the tendril, close winding
    The love, my heart binding,
Has left it all bleeding when torn from my side,

And my poor heart is grieving,
In sorrow bereaving,
Oh, why has she left me, my precious, my pride?

My baby, my treasure,
My well-spring of pleasure,
In Heaven thou'rt resting from sorrow and ill;
But thy mother's heart's breaking,
And all the while aching
And longing for Myla, whose place none can fill.

E'en though I be sinning
By ceaseless complaining,
The Lord will forgive, for my poor brain is wild.
Though the anguish I'm stilling,
I cannot be willing
To be severed fore'er from my darling, my child.

My heart, torn and bleeding,
Dear Father, is pleading,
I am lonely! so lonely; most saddening moan,
Its sorrow bereaving,
List to the heart grieving,
Oh, give back my darling, nor leave me alone!

### THE AWAKENING.

I thank thee this even,
Oh Father in Heaven ;
'Twas a horrible dream.   My darling is here,
With her smiles and caressing,
Close to my heart pressing ;
*Oh Father, I thank thee, I bless thee fore'er.*

So real the seeming
Of death in my dreaming,
Though gone is the dream, and unbroken our band,
Yet a moral 'tis teaching,
So many hearts reaching :
*Thank God all the while for the gifts from his hand.*

---

### WYANDOTTE.

MEMORIES, like tones, most sweetly ring,
And by their power a vision bring.
I see again that fairy grot
Within thy caverns, Wyandotte.

Thus memory's echo lingers long,
Like sweet refrain of soulful song,

3*

And then, oh joy, 'tis my blest lot
To see in dreams sweet Wyandotte.

And as the tones still rise and fall,
My heart responds to each and all ;
In future years my mind shall not
Forget thy realms, oh, Wyandotte.

Oft as sweet memories swell and rise,
They bring the moisture to my eyes ;
Thou'rt nature's child, without a blot
To mar thy beauty, Wyandotte.

At memory's touch my heart-strings thrill ;
Were I the creature of my will
I'd rest within an humble cot,
Beneath thy hillside, Wyandotte.

With thoughts of thee my mind doth teem,
My fancies float as in a dream,
For on this earth there is no spot
So dear to me as Wyandotte.

Thou'rt nature's child, and nature's lyre
Kindles the soul's ecstatic fire,
And never canst thou be forgot,
God's fairest work, dear Wyandotte.

June, 1873.

## NOBODY, NOBODY KNOWS.

WHO is it, then, that inspires my pen?
   Nobody, nobody knows.
It might be brother, or cousin ; but then,
   It is—none of those.

Who is it that claimeth my waking thought?
   Nobody, nobody knows.
Brothers or cousins—perhaps it ought
   To be some of those.

Who is it that visits me in a dream ?
   Nobody, nobody knows ;
So it ought, perhaps, but it does not seem
   Like any of those.

Who is it loves me above all the rest?
   Somebody, somebody knows ;
Brothers nor cousins could make me so blest,
   It is none of those.

Why is it he loves me?  Can ye tell ?
   Nobody, nobody knows ;
Why do I love him, canst say?  Ah ! well—
   He is not like those.

So shall we go loving on to the end?
   Nobody, nobody knows;
Brother nor cousin is he,—a friend
   Far dearer than those.

June, 1873.

---

# RONDEAU.

LET us love
While we may.
Land above,
Land of clay,
Do unite
Fair and bright;
Do meet
And complete,
In unions,
Communions—
Something sweet
Which we greet;
For its form,
Mid life's storm
Brings us hope,
Lifts us up
On its wings,
While it sings,

And with wiles
Care beguiles.
Thus our song,
Loud and long,
E'er the same
Bears the name
Of this dove.
Call it " Love"—
Thrills our heart,
Every part—
May it come
To its home,
Build its nest
In our breast,
Make us blest,
Love possessed.

# THE CHILD AND THE CONVICT.

Oh, prisoner with the weary air
    That seems an unbreathed sigh,
And brow marked o'er with furrowing care,
    And deep despondent eye,

What means the sudden look that gleams,
    Brightens thine eye with light,
That paints thy face with feeling—seems
    Like day-dawn after night?

What dost thou see?   A little child,
    Led by a mother's hand;
An infant girl in features mild
    Moves through this prison band.

This is the chord that touched thy heart
    And gave thine eye-beams birth,
This is the light of love, the part
    That glorifies the earth.

And, oh, that eager, yearning look!
    It thrills us like a tone;
We read it like a printed book,
    And it becomes our own.

We note the look of mute appeal,
　　Interpret as we ought;
We know, we think, we read, we feel,
　　We reach thy inmost thought.

Our hearts with kindred feelings swell;
　　We read with nature's art,
Thou hadst a child, thou know'st the spell
　　That thrills the father's heart.

Convict and stranger though thou art,
　　And outcast though thou be,
A little child can reach thy heart,
　　Show there pure thoughts to me.

———————

## THE POET.

My life may scatter sunbeams,
　　My face be smiling bright;
Yet in my heart there's sadness
　　That never seeks the light.

My life hath had its sorrows
　　Like chequered shadows cast;

They ever crossed my pathway,
   And will while life shall last.

Some joys erstwhile come to me,
   But pleasures never last ;
Except in thought they linger—
   In memories of the past.

I am no idle dreamer ;
   I work, I think, I feel.
Who chides me if, in rhyming,
   I may my thoughts reveal?

Some heavy-laden mortal,
   Who bows beneath his load,
Perhaps in reading my thoughts
   May firmer tread the road.

'Tis idle all repining ;
   Look up, be brave, be true :
Who knows but in the future
   Some brightness beams for you ?

Thus, while on earth I linger,
   I'll send forth words of cheer ;
For this, who knows, but may be
   My destined life-work here.

August, 1873.

# AGONY.

Friend, I have suffered since I saw thee last,
Yea, murderous aches and pains have passed
   My frame throughout.
   Still have I thought
If I could rest, that I at length
Might gather up my sorely wasted strength,
   And thus put pain to rout.

Why, I could point with sureness out, by pain alone,
Each nerve, or bone, or joint, each one.
   Dost ask me where
   My sufferings are?
I'll tell thee, friend, without reserve:
In this whole frame, where's joint, or bone, or nerve,
   *The pain is there !*

Thus every breath engenders pain severe,
And as I lie in suffering here,
   My inmost thought
   (Itself with pain is fraught)
Is, might I sleep,—sleep without breath,
E'en though I knew that silent sleep were death ;
   *I'd rather sleep than not.*

# INSANITY.

### A SKETCH.

I'M mad ; mad, mad ! I know but this—I'm mad !
My 'wildered brain doth ever seethe and boil
Like unto devil's broth in steaming caldron.
My mind is turmoil, and my thoughts are stirred
Into an endless maze of wild confusion,
And, as my fevered thoughts like misty vapors rise,
Or empty bubbles in uncertain flight,
I seek to reach, to guide and master them ;
Yet, ere I have the power, they vanish
Quick as meteor flash, and all is dark.
Another bubble riseth from my throbbing brain ;
Brightness gleams upon its wavering surface
As though the mind itself were shining through.
How eagerly ! ay, with what frantic haste
I try to grasp it ; but, alas, it bursts,
Resolves itself into airy nothingness,
Again I blindly grope in utter darkness.
These scintillating lights, bright bubbles from my mind
Do ever rise and vanish in their aimless way.
Their course through space is never pointed out :
No plans, no future destiny have they,

And thus to me they vividly portray
My madness.  And I know, I feel, I'm mad.
For what is madness ?   'Tis the power lost
To train these airy bubbles of the brain aright—
To follow up our thoughts, and still command,
Retain them as obedient servants.

But my mind hath had too many servants;
They have far too well filled their allotted sphere.
They throng the temple, and they crowd the brain ;
They beat upon the wall of mind, but ah, the wall
Gives way.   My mind is like a broken drum,
On which no echoing tones resound.
They surge and sway, in maddening glee, or harsh up-
     roar,
As ceaseless breakers of the sea dash on the rock-
     bound shore.

Yet they are strong; thoughts have become too strong.
They have o'erpowered me, and they are my masters.
I cannot, howe'er much I would, escape them,
And I, henceforth, like abject slave, or culprit whipped,
          Must do their bidding,
Although my weary step, wild eye, and haggard brow,
Prove how my strength is taxed beyond endurance.
Yet still these wicked thoughts like phantom forms
Do drive me on ; and whisper in my crazed ear,

Do this, do that, or yet the other ; thus they say,
And taunt and sneer and make me fiend inhuman ;
And though 'twere murder, suicide, or aught else,
I even must obey this mighty power,
This madness that hath me ever in its clutches,
As in the grip of Hercules, or massive iron vise,
From which no hand can save, no human help avail ;
From which no wrench, save that given by the hand of
    death,
              Can set my spirit free.

July, 1873.


# LINES TO G. C. H.


On, quivering, stricken heart, bowed down with sick-
    ening grief,
What earthly comfort may I bring, what words for thy
    relief?
For thee, my friend, the tear of sympathy must flow
Where there are hearts to feel or minds to picture half
    thy woe—

Who hath no ear to hear, no heart to feel another's
    woe,
Were even less than human.   But this fearful blow,

This wound, these pangs that rend thy heart, this
    dreadful evil
Who wouldst inflict 'twould seem were worse than
    fiend or devil.

Others ere this have known such anguished pain,
Have known, dread truth, may know and feel again.
Thy pride, the light that beamed within thy heart but
    late,
Flickered, and died, and darkened all thy life, now
    desolate.

Thy Flora, plunged in gulf of deep and dark despair,
Rushed madly to the ocean of eternity, and there
In presence of her Maker, while at his feet she kneels,
Her burdened soul its suffering; its wrongs, to Him
    reveals.

" I seek thy presence, Lord." " Why didst thou come?
Thou shouldst have waited patiently until I called thee
    home."
" I came unbidden, Father, for I thought, I felt, I
    must,
And I was not afraid of God, for God I knew was just.

" But 'twas the world I feared, the hard and cruel
    world,
For in my bleeding, wounded heart its poisonous darts
    were hurled ;

A lost lamb, I had strayed afar, in suffering untold—
Father, forgive me, though I sought to enter in thy
fold.

"I could not, Lord, remain on earth, to be a thing of
scorn,
Regretting, yea, and murmuring, that I had e'er been
born''—
And as she kneels with head low bowed before the great
white throne,
More sinned against than sinning, erring, repentant
one,

Methinks the voice of God is heard, a loving, sooth-
ing sound,
Falling in words of comfort, filled with balm to heal
thy wound :
"Daughter, thou art forgiven, and on earth, let him
alone
'Mong men, who is without sin, on thy memory cast a
stone.''

August 2', 1874.

# THE LONGING SOUL.

A BIRD imprisoned is my soul,
   That beats its bars in vain.
Ah, were it free, to heavenly goal
   'Twould soar from care and pain.

'Twould mount through azure depths so high,
   On free soul-freighted wing;
Above the clouds, beyond the sky,
   'Twould hear the angels sing.

Why seek true happiness below—
   On earth, where none is given?
Ah, yearning heart, dost thou not know
   Peace only dwells in heaven!

Oh longing soul! oh aching heart!
   Oh weary, tired brain,
Perform thy work, act well thy part—
   Thou, too, shalt rest from pain.

April, 1873.

## DARLING, THINK OF ME.

WHEN pleasure crowns thy pathway
   As sunset crowns the sea,
And all is joy and gladness,
   Then, darling, think of me.

In vista of the future,
   When promise rich thou'lt see,
Still in that hour remember,
   And, darling, think of me.

Should days of gloomy sorrow
   Their shadows cast o'er thee,
Yet, even then, remember,
   And sometimes think of me.

If in thy heart a yearning
   For kindred sympathy
Should swell that heart to bursting,
   My darling, think of me.

And oh, may all the brightness
   Of love be cast o'er thee;
Yet in thy love's fruition
   Sometimes you'll think of me.

For all must have their sorrows—
    A few may happy be ;
So then, in joy or sadness,
    Think kindly still of me.

In memory then will linger—
    Ah, linger lovingly—
In my heart thoughts of you, love,
    In your heart thoughts of me.

ıtember, 1873.

## MY SPIRIT TURNS TO THEE.

### A SONG.

Now let me whisper in thine ear !
    Most dear thou art to me.
In dreams I see thy form appear ;
    My spirit turns to thee—
        To thee,
    My spirit turns to thee.

Thy sweetness draws me on, dear one,
    As nectar draws the bee ;
As sunflower turns to greet the sun,
    My spirit turns to thee—
        To thee,
    My spirit turns to thee.

Thou art the fairest, dearest, best—
  To me shalt ever be,
I love them not, nor seek the rest—
  My spirit turns to thee—
      To thee,
  My spirit turns to thee.

Then doubt me not, nor fear to trust :
  My heart thou e'en shall see,
Look in my bosom, see thou must,
  My spirit turns to thee—
      To thee,
  My spirit turns to thee.

September, 1873.


# FAREWELL.

Farewell, friend, and though forever
  We may tread life's ways apart,
Time or distance ne'er can sever
  Bonds of friendship from the heart.

Wheresoe'er my footsteps linger—
  Hill or vale or sounding sea,
All their beauties would be dearer
  Still, my friend, if shared with thee.

Nature's silent sweet communion
  Kindred thoughts within us thrill,
And our minds in kindred union
  Join, unmindful of our will.

Let our thoughts remain unspoken—
  Words but hide the thought away—
Nature's silence be unbroken
  Only by the breath of May.

Kindly thoughts within us teeming,
  Purest joy on earth we find;
Sympathetic throbs of feeling
  Stir the heart and sway the mind.

Nature's pictures true are dearer
  When they thrill a kindred heart;
But I may not have thee nearer,
  For our paths lie wide apart.

Farewell, friend, and should we never
  Meet again, for now we part,
May I hope that thou wilt ever
  Hold remembrance in thy heart?

PEPERELL, Mass., May, 1874.

## THAT ALL MAY JUDGE.

In caustic wit, while some may fail,
Before the Judge all others pale.
Ah! would that wit included praise,
Which but a censuring thought displays;
For hidden satire lurks beneath
Bland words, which form a flowery wreath.
Expressions soft from smiling lip,
Like gloved hand, hide a painful grip.
Ah! that the Judge, so great in mind,
In judgment were a trifle kind ;
And being Judge, full well he must
Fulfill his part—be not unjust,
Nor malice prepense hold should he—
The Judge and I might then agree.
I much admire his sparkling wit,
Or manly, upright "shoulder hit,"
And surely no one should object
To greet the power of intellect,
For brilliant thoughts we like to see,
And mark the ready repartee;
E'en irony might not be bad,
If one were only iron-clad,

But caustic wit none can admire,
You know "a burned child dreads the fire."
Advice from him would many ask
If that were not a dreadful task;
For much they have a shrinking fear
Of cutting words that they might hear.
For rather give a "cut direct"
Than cutting words for mere effect;
It does require a deal of nerve
To take the thing we least deserve.
The tender plant asks gentle touch
Or suffers.   Does it ask too much?
In all his "charges" right and just
A judge should be, will be, I trust.
There is a mantle pure and fair
Which each and all of us should wear.

Judge this, not by the general rule,
That every poet is a fool;
For though he be or be not *smart*,
He still, my friend, may have a heart;
If poets lack sometimes in sense,
Their sense-itiveness is immense.
They suffer from the chilling blast
Of sarcasm, ever sweeping past.
The tender plant asks gentle touch
Or suffers—'tis not asking much:

From lamb that's shorn the wind we shield;
The heart's laid bare, its thoughts revealed;
A store of thought and feelings true,
Pure pearls, the poet brings to you.
Be careful of the tender thought,
Or all its wealth avails you naught;
The gold that's hidden under ground,
Is for a purpose, coined, when found;
So hidden wealth of heart and mind
Is coined in words to help mankind;
A tender thought expression given
Does sometimes bring us nearer heaven.
A writer may his duty do
If to himself and others true,
And he who feels his motive pure
Much good may do, much ill endure.
If ye have talent, then, deserve;
By use its shine undimmed preserve,
Of others' feelings have a care,
Yet in the right just do and dare.
Than these no truer thoughts were wed:
" Be sure you're right," and " go ahead ;"
And surely none there is but knows
The gold that's rubbed the brighter grows.
Talent, though sometimes much abused,
Bright lustre sheds when rightly used,
God gives us talent that we may
Its strength increase from day to day,

Nor let rust its bright surface dim,
But let its light reflect on Him.
Prosperity I envy none
No more than star might envy sun ;
All may not in its sunshine bask—
Some of us work a life-long task—
And seldom is it that we hear
Kind words of praise or words of cheer,
Which make our life-work somewhat light,
And e'en the future seem more bright.
But justice should not be denied,
The Court should not the law o'erride.
The golden rule did all apply
How few would then for justice cry.
The "Judge is just," then let him feel
The truth set forth in this appeal,
And let him not, whate'er he do,
Another's motive misconstrue.
Derision I would not excite,
A just decision I invite ;
I may not climb the hill of Fame ;
Justice and truth is all I claim,
Nor praise nor censure I bespeak,
" Justice to all" is all I seek.

September, 1873.

# THE GLORIOUS FOURTH.

PROCLAIM it o'er earth—
No more the oppressor's hand
Shall smite our beauteous land;
In Freedom now we stand.
    All hail!   The Glorious Fourth!

The day of freedom's birth,
Reaching from sea to sea,
Our land to-day is free—
Thus evermore to be.
    All hail!   The Glorious Fourth!

East, West, and South, and North,
Take up the glad refrain
And sound it o'er again,
Throughout our wide domain.
    All hail!   The Glorious Fourth!

The Stars and Stripes bring forth,
And to the breezes fling!
We'll wave them while we sing,
And make the welkin ring.
    All hail!   The Glorious Fourth!

To freedom, joy, and mirth,
We dedicate this day,
And fitting tribute pay ;
Be this our roundelay—
    All hail !   The Glorious Fourth!

July 4, 1875.

---

# HYMN.

[*Tune*, " Maid of Athens."]

In this, the temple of thy word
We meet to sing thy praises, Lord,
Like manna to the penitent
Thy gracious promises are sent.
Guide us aright, make clear our sight,
Guide us aright, make clear our sight,
Oh, Lord of mercy, Lord of love !
Oh, Lord of mercy, Lord of love !
    Look down from Heaven above.

Keep us in straight and narrow way,
Oh, never may our footsteps stray.
Teach us to do Thy holy will,
Help us Thy mandates to fulfill,

5*

Incline Thine ear, oh, deign to hear!
Incline Thine ear, oh, deign to hear,
And from Thy sacred throne on high
And from Thy sacred throne on high
And from Thy sacred throne on high
    Oh, list the sinner's cry!

Redeemer, Brother, Saviour, Friend!
To Thee our grateful prayers ascend;
Be Thou with us, whate'er betide;
For us, our Saviour crucified.
Teach us in youth the living truth;
Teach us in youth the living truth;
Then shall our ransomed souls arise,
Then shall our ransomed souls arise,
Then shall our ransomed souls arise
    To dwell in Paradise.

To Thee a faltering voice we raise;
In trembling tones we sing Thy praise.
When all our earthly songs are done
We with the angels round Thy throne
Oh, Lord of love,—in Heaven above
Oh, Lord of love,—in Heaven above
In newer, sweeter tones may sing,
In newer, sweeter tones may sing,
In newer, sweeter tones may sing
    Thy praises, Heavenly King.

## TO MY SON.

DARE to do right, dare to be strong,
As on life's highway you journey along,
Dare to do good, be honest and true,
So shall a blessing be meted to you.

Dare to do right, my own darling boy,
Thy heart and mine will be laden with joy;
Dare to do right, be not afraid,
Lend to the helpless and needy thine aid.

Dare to do right, dare to be brave,
From sorrow and danger seek others to save;
Shun ever the wine-cup, dare to say No,
In path that you traverse some other may go.

Dare to do right, dare to say Yes,
Such a reply may some weary heart bless;
Be hopeful and brave till thy journey is done:
With daring and courage life's battles are won.

Dare to do right; may thy course, like the lark,
Be onward and upward and true to the mark.
May faith, hope, and love bright beacon-lights
    prove,
To guide thee in safety to heaven above.

# THE MAY-QUEEN.

QUEEN of the May,
Beautiful May,
Blithesome and mirthful and joyous and gay;
Scatter wild flowers,
Spring-time's fair flowers,
How they beguile many wearisome hours!

Never was seen
Velvet so green,
As the grass where we hail thee our beauteous queen;
Bright is the day,
Joyous our play,
Happiest, brightest, the queen of the May.

# THE FIRE-FIEND.

'Tɪs a Sabbath evening fair,
Peaceful quiet all the air
  Does pervade, does prepare
Every heart, and the chime
Of the church-bell says 'tis time
  For the hour of prayer.

Church-bells now have ceased to ring.
Hushed and still is everything;
  Holy quiet peace doth bring
To the heart and soul most near—
Peace to one and all most dear
  Round the heart doth cling.

Suddenly there sounds a cry
As of peril coming nigh.
  Whence the sound and what the cry,
What the danger, what the harm,
Menaced in that wild alarm?
  Tell us, passer-by.

Now 'tis coming, nigher, nigher,
Hark, the cry is "fire! fire!"
  Speeding fast by magic wire

The alarm flies to the tower,
Then the clanging bells join in ;
Sound of hurrying, clang, and din
Rises higher still and higher,
　　Like the raging fire.

Engines now and men so brave
Put forth all their power to save,
　　And each burning building lave,
Drench and flood with water.
Fiery heat still waxes hotter ;
Still the men work harder, faster ;
But the fire still is master,
　　Man is but its slave.

Toughest hose like bubbles burst,
Does the heat not melt it first.
　　Surely, fire, thou art accurst ;
Truth of gloom and melancholy,
Seems as though to strive were folly ;
On the mind is forced,
　　Bravest men are served the worst.

What is water, earth, or air?
How can each or all compare,
　　Or in battle can they dare,
Rank above or equal fire?

Emulous but vain desire,
   They may not compare.

See it leaping, dancing, creeping,
Through the doors and windows leaping ;
   What cares fire, though men be weeping
O'er the loss of wealth and power,
Swept from grasp within the hour,
   Swept by fire as now 'tis sweeping.

Iron fronts are forward bending,
Toppling walls are downward tending ;
   Their fall a thrill of awe is sending
To each heart—and over all
Cloud of flame and smoke does fall,
   Added grandeur lending.

Still the men in vain endeavor,
Like a power without a lever,
   Strive in fruitless, vain endeavor
To conquer, conquer Fire.
Vain attempts and vain desire ;
Now the wind is rising higher,
Reinforcement to the fire,
   Conquering now or never.

Heat intense and smoke as black
As Egypt's midnight drive men back ;
   Must they fail ?  Alack, alack—

Brave and true and faithful still ;
Nerves of steel, and iron will,
Do.their hopes at last fulfill, —
   Cause the fire to slack.

Now the wind is sobbing, sighing,
For the fire at last is dying
   Mid its smouldering ruins lying ;
Fiercest flames are backward driven ;
Fire's death-blow has been given,
   Therefore, wind, thy sighing.

Grandest glory has King Fire,
Mingling in his funeral pyre,
   Arches, roofs, and lordly hall,
   Iron front and massive wall,
   Hanging black smoke over all
   Like a mighty funeral pall,
O'er destruction dire,
Handwork of King Fire.

March, 1874.

# WAITING.

Waiting for thought-buds to spring at my bidding,
To blossom in beautiful flowers of rhyme ;
Though their beauty enchanting
Is lost by transplanting
From my mind to this page, far more rigorous clime.

Waiting for visions that live in my mem'ry
To step from their prison, stand fair to the view,
And tell the brave story,
How one mortal's glory
Was to ever be hopeful and loving and true.

Waiting for one who to me should be hast'ning ;
Waiting and watching and hoping again.
Ah ! sure, did he love me,
He would not thus prove me.
Alas, weary heart, thou art waiting in vain !

Waiting for trials and storms that come sweeping ;
Life's shadows and sorrows, like thickening gloom,
Aye, gather around us,
Until they surround us,—
Our only escape seems a welcoming tomb.

# LOVE'S FOUNT.

STRAY your feet
To love's fount; may you bring
  In your heart love to me,
    Nectar sweet!
Let us taste, let us sing,
  As in tasting we see
    Joy complete!

  Do you think
Such a nectar would pall
  On the taste, or the heart
    Cease to drink
At love's fount, unheeding love's call,
  From love's sweetness depart
    At the brink?

  Can you guess?
In this fount is a spell,
  For a thrill like a tone
    Does possess
Those who drink at love's well;
  Nectar sip, love's alone,
    Love's caress!

Love divine
Thrills our hearts as we sip,
   And we feel love possessed.
      'Thou art mine ;
      I am  thine ;
''Tis nectar we quaff from the lip ;
   Kisses sweet, rapture blest
      With love's wine !


   Like a dove,
In the heart perfect bliss
   Finds a home.   Swell our song
      Far above
Other songs.   Love's first kiss,
   Tremulous, thrilling and long,
      Kiss of  love !


   Perfect bliss
In the heart, like a dove,
   Finds a home :  perfect rest.
      Who would miss
      Joy like this,
Of a heart filled with love ?
   Oh, the rapture expressed
      In love's kiss !

# THOUGHTS OF THEE.

AT memory's touch my heart-strings thrill.
Were I the creature of my will,
Did all my future rest with me,
I'd share it, brave, true friend, with thee,—
　　　　True friend, with thee.

With thoughts of thee my mind doth teem;
My fancies float as in a dream;
For thou, my friend, art dear to me,
And love sends love's sweet thoughts to thee—
　　　　Sweet thoughts to thee.

Thou'rt nature's child, and nature's lyre
Kindles the soul's ecstatic fire
Of love.　Oh, would that I might be
Where rests my heart,—that is, with thee!—
　　　　That is, with thee.

So thoughts of thee still swell and roll
A flood of rapture o'er my soul:
Is rapture wrong? or canst thou see
'Tis wrong to love one like to thee,—
　　　　One like to thee?

## LOVE'S INVOCATION.

MAY your life
Be as bright
As the sun's
Beam of light !
May your dreams
Happy be !
May you see
Only me
When you wake.
Darling one,
Time to come,
Pleasure fraught,
Let your song,
Sweet and long,
Float above,
Song of love,
Love possessed,
We are blessed
With love-light
Clear and bright.
Darling one,
As the sun

And its ray
Guides our way,
Every day
Leads us on ;
Leads us up
Far beyond
Lesser clay,
Till we meet
And we greet
In the land
Up above,—
Land of love.

———

## THE OCEAN OF LIFE.

No more, no more on ocean's shore we'll stand,
Watching the wild waves greet and kiss the land,
Nor gather shells upon the pebbly shore,
No more, my friend ; ah, never, never more !

We sail away.   Upon life's ocean wide
Our barks are moving onward with the tide ;
Perchance somewhere on ocean's wide domain,
Sailing along, we all may meet again.

Heaven's breeze fills the sails for the voyage of life
Through waves of despair or breakers of strife;
Truth pilots our boat past the shoals of deceit;
Were't not for her guidance they'd wreck us complete.

Our true hearts are brave. Hope, buoyant and strong,
Bears the anchor as we float along;
She whispers a promise that zephyrs and tide
Will waft us to safety as onward we glide.

Faith, looking beyond, through the clouds of life's sky,
Bids us be of good cheer though danger be nigh;
And love's at the helm, the vessel to steer
To a haven of bliss;—we have nothing to fear.

But our sails are set; we are floating away,
And wide, wide apart our fragile barks stray.
In heaven, when storms and dangers be past,—
In a haven of rest may Hope's anchor be cast!

CONEY ISLAND, May, 1874.

# IN MEMORIAM.—LITTLE HORACE.

### INSCRIBED TO MRS. A. E. FLETCHER.

Thou hadst a shining pearl,
A fairy child, with floating golden curl,
 A gem that erst was thine.
Now, lifted up to heaven's light,
Thy pearl hath grown more pure, more bright,
 And shines with light divine.

Thou hadst a beauteous gem,—
A rosebud, clinging to its parent stem
 From dewy morn till even.
Yet from its stem the bud was torn ;
Thy heart, alas ! is left to mourn,—
 Thy rosebud blooms in heaven.

Thou hadst a little bird
Whose thrilling notes were sweetest ever heard ;
 It nestled in thy breast
Away from care and sin.
Heaven's portal ope'd,—thy bird flew in,
 Thy heart's an empty nest.

Thou hadst, oh heart oppressed,
A lamb; 'tis folded on the Shepherd's breast:
    Away from pain and strife,
Where sorrow cannot come,
Thy lamb hath found a safer home,
    And purer, better life.

Thou hadst a prattling child,
Than which none fairer, sweeter, ever smiled:
    Too pure, too fair, for earth.
It lingered little while to bless
Thy heart, whose yearning tenderness
    Through suffering finds new birth.

Thy soul must e'en look up,
Though to the dregs thou'st drained the bitter cup;
    Look up through clouds of grief.
Faith looks through tears to light above,
For God is e'er a God of love,
    And He will bring relief.

May, 1875.

# IN MEMORIAM.

### D. B. CHARLES.

I AM sitting beside thy grave, darling,
  'Neath the tree near its grassy green mound ;
The murmuring breeze through the leaves, darling,
  In my heart wakes responsive resound.

In spirit you whisper to me, darling,
  As you beckon me ever to come ;
And footprints of time on life's path, darling,
  Lead on to a heavenly home.

Then followed my life's darkest night, darling,
  With never a starlight's faint gleam,
And I could not rouse from the thrall, darling,
  Seeming so like a horrible dream.

Many years have gone by since then, darling,
  Many sorrows passed over my head,
Since I took up life's burden again, darling,
  With hope, not unmingled with dread.

I linger again in the past, darling,
  'Midst the joys and the scenes long agone,
Ere Fate's ruthless hand struck the blow, darling,
  That left me to struggle alone.

With death's icy chill on your brow, darling,
  When my heart was rebellious, you said,
"'Tis His will; God knows best." Oh, my darling!
  Yet thou liest low with the dead.

But "He knoweth best," so you said, darling,
  And I bowed to the chastening rod ;
Were it not for our pledges of love, darling,
  I, too, would have slept 'neath the sod.

But life had a duty for me, darling,
  The walk to the distaff I tread ;
'Tis the path of a duty to do, darling,
  Reweaving my life's broken thread.

---

## THE KISS AND TEAR.

IF untold bliss
Lurks in a kiss,
There's something more endears ;
More precious far
Than kisses, are
The welling, heart-felt tears.

Who nectar sips
From dewy lips,
Would find a fount more dear,
If they who'd snatch
A kiss, would catch
The dearer, falling tear.

Love-light we prize
Beams in the eyes,
The sense of joy most dear ;
Love's purest glance,
Tear-drops enhance,
The silent, unchecked tear.

The memory
Of sympathy
Shines through the mist of years ;
As light that dies
In sunset skies
Shines through the rain-drops' tears.

When I am glad,
Or when I'm sad,
I'll bring thee what endears ;
It lies in this :
The chastened bliss,
The tenderness of tears.

'Twere sweet to rest
On faithful breast,
And cast aside all fears;
There bring the bliss
Of love's pure kiss,
There find relief in tears.

When stilly death,
With chilly breath,
Shall quell heart-throbs and fears,
Then o'er my brow—
Oh, why not now?—
Thou'lt shed affection's tears.

And shouldst thou miss
The loving kiss,
That memory still reveres;
Then lingers yet
This fond regret,
I might have caught her tears!

# TO THE HAPPIEST MAN IN TOWN.

THEY say thou art happy!   How little they know
What silent sorrow, what unuttered woe,
May burden thy heart till it sinketh in grief;
And it seemeth no power can bring thee relief.

That sad yearning longing, that nameless unrest,
Like the low bending head, hopeless waits to be blest;
Shall the heart never rest?   Yes, beyond the blue sky;
Thy longing shall reach it, perhaps, by and by.

A gay peal of laughter as merry words flow
Is the surface, that covers grief hidden below;
And the careless tone which to jesting we lend
Is the froth, cast aside, when the heart finds a friend.

So revelry, mirth, the cares of the world,
Or the battle of life, where our flag is unfurled,
But hide weary heart-aches, and deaden the tone
Of the inward sorrow, and silence its moan.

Thy heart seemeth lightsome and glad all the day,
And revels in mirth, as the lambkins at play;
Yet those who have suffered its wailing have heard,
Like the sad complaint of lone mourning bird.

A well-spring lies hidden in every heart,
At sympathy's touch its current may start ;
'Tis a pearly depth, with tear-drops 'tis fraught,
That flow from the fountain of pure loving thought.

The pain and the anguish we bravely endure,
Though the heart seemeth riven, they make it more
       pure.
Thou shalt reap the reward after wearisome years,
And harvest sweet thought where ye sowed bitter tears.

And hopes will spring up when ye thought all had died,
As Christ rose in glory though first *crucified*,
Send thy thoughts upward, thy heart bid rejoice,
There love finds expression, and longing a voice.

And sorrow's ennobling, ingratitude smarts,
But it makes us prize highly the o'erflowing hearts,—
The pure, deep heart-throb we, stifling, conceal,
Love, truth, and tenderness few know or feel.

They say thou art happy as butterfly bright,
And seemingly thoughtless of time's wingèd flight ;
Should care come and heart-aches (which Heaven fore-
       fend !),
And thou need true sympathy, seek thou—
                  Thy friend.

# A SIGH.

A BEAUTIFUL day
Seems a mockery
When the heart is o'ershadowed with grief.
As the hours slowly fly,
Or the moments creep by,
In our sorrow we cry,
Oh, time, on thy wings bring relief!

Only sorrow and fears
They bring us, the years,
Which we hoped would be laden with love;
And our heart, it appears,
Floats in deluge of tears,
Till Hope's messenger-dove
The olive-leaf, Peace, finds above.

CHRISTMAS, 1874.

# MY DARLING.

WHAT shall I say to my darling, my darling?
　　What shall I bring to my love?
　　What that a blessing shall prove?—
　　　A sunbeam of morning,
　　　A halo adorning
　　The heart, I will bring to my love.

What shall I say to my darling, my darling?
　　What shall I bring to my love?
　　　A rapture most sweet,
　　　A joy most complete,
　　　It is fitting and meet
　　That with love I should bring to my love.

What shall I say to my darling, my darling?
　　What shall I bring to my love?
　　　A heart full of feeling,
　　　Its love unconcealing,
　　　Its homage revealing,—
　　All these will I bring to my love.

February 14, 1875.

7*

# THOUGHT.

Oh, thought! that is deeper and vaster
  Than the cavernous depth of the sea,
I will still be of artists the master,
  And portray an ideal of thee.

Sweet lips that are dewy and tender
  As the soft budding heart of the rose,
Bright eyes, filled with deepening splendor,
  While musing o'er them my thought grows.

'Neath the lips, pearly gems whitely gleaming,—
  Cheeks, the lily, the rose, and the down,—
The brow, pure and fair, 'twould be seeming
  To crown with a matronly crown.

In the depth of the eye now is glowing
  A smile, or a tear-drop, I see;
Through them the sweet image is showing
  A pictured idea to me.

I am sure 'tis provoking and shocking!
  I essayed not to picture a group,
Yet see how the thoughts will come flocking,—
  'Stead of one thought here comes a whole troop.

Now in sadness and deep lamentation
   I demolish the daub I had wrought;
Humbly seeking a new avocation,
   I will work in the garden of thought.

I will labor and cease all complaining.
   Thought still makes my life-work sublime,
For her rosebuds shall bloom by my training
   Into beautiful flowers of rhyme.

# THE PROPHET AND THE MOUNTAIN.

### A QUERY.

THE truth I will seek in a query,
   While I gaze in the depths of thine eyes;
Thinkest thou that Mahomet was very
   Remarkably, wondrously wise?

Though a journey he took to a mountain,
   Perchance there to breathe out his sighs,
Like bubbles thrown off by the fountain,
   Yet, say, does that prove he was wise?

Now I ask you in all truth and candor,—
    For falsehood's a cheat I despise,—
To the foot of the mount though he'd wander,
    In that can you think he was wise?

But the mountain would come to him never,—
    At least so methinks some one cries,—
Though he longed for it ever and ever,
    So, perhaps, it may be he was wise.

You and I, just to strengthen my meaning,
    May the mountain and prophet comprise;
Though the one to the other is leaning,
    Yet, say, can you think it is wise?

To the mountain the prophet draws nearer,
    And it may not occasion surprise
Should each to the other grow dearer,
    Yet, I fear me, 'tis not very wise.

The mountain is reached, and together
    Their brows they uplift to the skies,
Communing with nature,—but whether,
    Say, whether *our* prophet is wise?

## EVA'S BIRTHDAY PRESENT.

LITTLE Eva, darling child,
Thy fair face hath me beguiled;
From thine eyes of lovely hue
Glorious soul is shining through.

"Twelve years old," I heard thee say,—
Life-thread twelve years long to-day;
Ah! the years go quickly past,
Wingèd milestones fly so fast.

May thy path be strewn with flowers!
May thy days bring golden hours!
May no trouble dim thy sky!
Only silver clouds float by.

Mayst thou, through the coming years,
Traverse not the vale of tears!
May, when quite to woman grown,
Nature's guide be still thine own!

Nature's grace, so free and simple,
Wrap it 'round thee like a mantle;
Nature's beauty, child-like grace,
Studied art can ne'er replace.

All I have to thee I send,
Birthday present from thy friend ;
Only this—a Hawthorn blossom :
Wear it ever on thy bosom.

Flower of " Hope," with magic power,
To light thy path through darkest hour ;
"Hope" I give thee, hoping never
Thou wilt cease to love the giver.

When our book of life shall close,
When we sleep in death's repose,
When our days shall close in even,
Hope we then to meet in heaven.

LOGANSPORT, June 6, 1875.

---

## THE TWO GIFTS.

HE gave me first a golden pen in pearly-tinted case,
The ready scribe, the weapon-guide, that with my
    thoughts keep pace ;
A pen well wielded, surer far and mightier than the
    sword,
Should write the loving tender thought in ever-living
    word ;

And yet no precious word nor thought would this gold
    pen indite
Until he gave me flowers fair,—they taught me what to
    write ;
The second gift, the flowers rare, with fragrance all
    were fraught,
And leafy vine and tendrils twine among their sprays
    were wrought.

Then woke the sleeping buds of thought that grow in
    heart and mind,
And vines of love and tenderness that with them inter-
    twined.
The pen that is controlled by thought may richest joy
    impart,
When flowers of friendship spring to bloom in garden
    of the heart.

Unfading flowers of friendship pure are never cast
    aside,
As sweet perfume of leafy June their fragrance will
    abide.
Whene'er I wish a pleasant word or message to indite,
Love, truth, and friendship guide my pen and teach
    me what I write.

# THE WITHERED MYRTLE (LOVE BETRAYED.)

### AN ACROSTIC.*

FRIEND, early on thy brow was a withered myrtle placed,

Closely "nettles" hedged thee in, for scandal thee embraced.

A monkshood's "poisonous words,"—with these the air was rife,

And ruthless nightshades of "suspicion" hovered o'er thy life.

A "disappointed hope" the cypress brought, and also dark despair.

E'en like bright flowers thy future looked, yet flowers may hide a snare,

A pure white poppy's ever fraught with either "good or ill;"

And thee, ah, friend! 'twas doomed to heal, though healing it did kill.

---

* To find the name hidden in this acrostic, take the first letter of the first line in connection with the second letter of the second line, the third letter of the third line, the fourth letter of the fourth, and so on, when the name will thus appear—Flora K. Harding.

Yet one more floral offering on thy memory's grave I
    lay,
While beside that grave most earnestly and fervently I
    pray
That all with thee is well.  Let these my offerings be,
First Hawthorn blossoms only, yet they "hope in-
    voke" for thee,
And a name wrought out in flowers with the thread of
    poesy.

---

## LINES TO H. P. B.

Now, after many years of life well spent,
              Art thou at length content ?

Thou shouldst be happy, for thy fame
Has spread abroad.  Is that the aim
Of happiness, or does she dwell
Unknown, in quiet, in thy breast?
Dost thou e'er suffer and yet say 'tis well
That I with care and grief should be oppressed?
Is there no wish unsatisfied, no yearning quelled,
No clinging hope destroyed, no boon from thee with-
    held?

If thou dost dwell with love, and hope, and peace,
Ah! then, my friend, thy life is full of bliss.

In time past thou hast sorrowed; pity then
The suffering of one—that one thy friend
Till death.   My path through life is rough, and when
I upward strive, I fall.   Put forth thy helping hand
To guide my steps.   I have no staff, no prop
On which to lean.   One moment stop
And listen to my pleading.   Wilt thou be
A friend in need, to counsel and encourage me,
So thy kind tones their every word shall cheer,
And bind me to thee with a tie most dear?

Few flowers, though I love flowers, brighten my path-
    way now;
Few rays of sunshine light my darkened, shadowed
    brow;
The promised rainbow of my hope appears
A mockery to my weary eyes, flooded with tears.
A yearning, tired aching fills my breast;
Unceasing sorrow will not let me rest.
Ah, me! yet I must bravely hope and struggle on,
Till all my earthly tasks are done,—
Until, like thee, the goal of peace I've won.

February, 1875.

# THE MAY MORNING.

'TWAS a beautiful morning in May,
   I sadly was musing the while;
The sun sent his beams out to play,
   Earth's face was reflecting God's smile.

To my soul then there whispered a voice,
   Saying, Thou, too, shalt win the reward;
Look up through thy tears and rejoice;
   Believe and have faith in the Lord.

Storms of grief gather over thee fast;
   Still onward, press on to thy goal.
Sorrow's clouds still surround, nor go past;
   Thou canst still soar above, wingèd soul.

Cast aside all thy doubtings and fears,
   Though darkness o'ershadow thy way,
Dark paths through long, wearisome years,
   Must lead to a glorious day.

Press on till thou seest the light;
   Soon, soon will the darkness be gone,
For daylight e'er follows the night,
   And 'tis darkest before the day-dawn.

With that beautiful morning in May
    Came this lesson,—I'm learning it now,—
And the whisper still seemeth to say,
    'Tis a blessing I breathe o'er thy brow.

## MAN AND THE BEE.

To sum it all up and take man at the best,
He is like to the bee, which is never at rest,
    But culling the sweets from every fair flower;
Like that woodland rover, he's e'er on the wing,
Gathering honey and leaving a sting.

And he careth no more than a thoughtless boy
Cares for his broken and thrown-away toy:
    It has served his purpose, beguiled a dull hour;
But he tires of it soon, and away he will fling,
Though it once gave him pleasure, the now worthless
        thing.

The bee, and the boy, and the man are the same:
Each play the same part in life's checkered game,
    In woodland, or play-room, or fair lady's bower;
The flower and the toy is the womanly heart
Rifled, broken, or stung, left to suffer and smart.

Oh ! are there no sweets that never will cloy ?
And is there no love that is ever a joy,
    Forever asserting its God-given power ?
No deep human tenderness still to inspire,
And lead us and teach us to still come up higher ?

October, 1874.

## WHAT I ASK FOR.

I ASK not for riches, for riches are fleeting ;
    We can buy not the joys which we sigh for in vain ;
Wealth may drive away happiness, a ruin completing,
    As dreams that have vanished come never again.

I ask not for honors as high as the eyrie,
    Where eaglet doth hover.   Even majesty's crown
May encircle a brow that is aching and weary,
    And finds no repose on a pillow of down.

I ask not for passion, for passions alarm me,
    Though the vials are emptied and poured at my feet.
May passion's emotion of life never harm me !
    Its breath is the simoon ; its storm, pelting sleet.

I ask not for fame,—an ethereal vapor,
    As empty, as airy, as fleeting is fame,—

8*

A flickering light from a ha'penny taper :
  Reflects but a moment, and dies with a name.

I ask not gay pleasure,—a beautiful bubble,
  But hollow and fleeting, most worthless of all.
It bursts o'er one's head, making no end of trouble.
  Entice me not, pleasure, I heed not your call.

But give me contentment, whatever my station,
  Whatever my sorrow, wherever my lot,
For it casts o'er the soul rays of pure elevation,
  Though it gleam in the palace or brighten the cot.

And give me a heart full of generous feeling,
  Of kindliest love and affection for all,
With sympathy stored and its love unconcealing,—
  A heart that responds to humanity's call.

And give me a mind that is strong, yet forbearing,—
  As wise as a serpent, as pure as a dove ;
A mind that is thoughtful, and noble, and daring,
  That soars on the pinions of heavenly love.

In this sorrowing world give me friends that are leal,—
  Friends in need for my own, that are honest and
      true
Through sunshine and shadow, when woe comes or weal.
  Such gifts are so rare I will ask but a few.

January, 1875.

# THE STATUE.

I stand on a base of common sense,—
A firm foundation with which to commence ;
A bud of Genius is in my hand,
To bloom, perhaps, in a better land.
My brow is crowned with the flowers of love,
A priceless gift from heaven above ;
But, ah ! their fragrance makes me human.
I wake, I weep, I am—a woman.

# THE OFFERING.

From the world I tread a little apart,
  Through the path that leads to my king ;
To him, all the wealth of my womanly heart
  Is the priceless treasure I bring.

The casket is stored with pearls of thought,
  That grew from heart-wounds and tears,
Gathered in suffering, patiently sought
  In the sands of the by-gone years.

And it holdeth a gem as a diamond bright,—
  'Tis the purest of earthly love :
It lendeth to darkness a radiant light,
  As the stars that are beaming above.

Ah ! can he reject such a peerless gift,
  Or can he my offering disdain ?
At his feet lies the treasure ; the casket I lift,
  Now 'tis heavy with aching pain.

June, 1875.

## IMPROMPTU.

My thoughts are little singing birds,
  That ever fly to thee ;
If I their carols put in words,
  'Tis thus I set them free.

If thy heart-thoughts are other birds
  That struggle to be free,
Unloose their pinions, give them words,
  And let them fly to me.

Extract from a letter, May, 1875.

# THE LESSON.

TEACH me, teach me how to love thee,
  Teach me how to win thy love;
Not the sun that shines above thee
  Than my joy would brighter prove.

Teach me, teach me how to love thee,
  Teach me how to tell my love;
Teach my thoughts to sway and move thee,
  Floating on the breath of love:

Teach me not, I know I love thee,
  Teach me not to tell, my love.
Now my spirit bends above thee,
  Sweet, receive my treasure-trove.

None there are I prize above thee,
  None whom I so dearly love.
If thou canst not say, " I love thee,"
  Oh, believe not that I love !

May, 1875.

# TO MISS HATTIE WISNER.

Of all the sweet lassies and all the dear cousins,
Though I love them so dearly and count them by dozens,
'Tis for her I most care, for none may compare
With my dear cousin Hattie, so good and so fair.

Her black eyes mean mischief; her hair hangs in curls,
And for making you happy she beats all the girls.
If her you should see, I'm sure that, like me,
In love with this bright peerless maiden you'd be.

Her voice is as clear as the clear rippling rill;
Her notes are as pure as the tones of a bell.
Like a siren she'll charm; may nothing e'er harm
My bonnie bright Hattie down east on the farm !

I'd tell you how winsome she is, if I could,
How graceful and witty, and handsome and good ;
And love her I do, and so, too, would you,
If only this bonnie sweet maiden you knew.

PEPPERELL, MASS., June, 1874.

## TO NETTIE MERRILL, OF BROOK-LYN.

### WRITTEN IN HER ALBUM.

Now what shall I say to thee, Annette,
Annette my darling, Annette my pet?
Shall I speak of the azure depth of thine eyes,
(May never a tear to their fair surface rise!)
Of thy cheeks like the rose,
Of that *retrousse* nose,
Or the half-hidden beauties thy dimples disclose?
Nay, nay, I tell thee, I'll write no such stuff,
I'll say but, "I love thee."   Is that not enough?
But that thou art handsome my last line will prove—
*We see every beauty in those whom we love.*


## HEART-YEARNINGS.

A SAD-EYED maid with care oppressed
  Sought one to tell her grief;
To let her tears fall on his breast
  Would bring such sweet relief.

With overflowing eyes she sought
　　One whom she loved near by ;
Seeing her tears, he said he thought
　　*'Twould do her good to cry.*

So true her love, her heart averred,
　　He'd fold her to his breast,
And she would, like a little bird,
　　Weave in his heart her nest.

" He could not, though he'd like," he said,
　　" The falling shower of grief
Catch on his breast,"—he brought instead
　　A—*pocket-handkerchief.*

She hoped he'd take her to his heart,
　　Dispelling grief and care,
Say, " Here's thy home, shun sportsman's art,
　　Hide here from fowler's snare."

For thus to him her love went forth,
　　'Twas his, 'twas freely given ;
The loving thought should ne'er had birth,
　　Her fondest hopes are riven.

Her tears, he said, were pearls of thought
　　That crown the poet's brow,
Yet they must flow by him uncaught ;
　　Therefore she's weeping now.

# INDICTED, CONVICTED, AND SEN-TENCED.

You say you have oft been *indited*,
　　Which "indictment" I think may be true;
'Tis meet now if I have the power,
　　That I bring a "conviction" to you.

This writing the silent witness
　　Will the proof of your guilt impart;
This *inditement* convicts you a felon,
　　For it proves you have stolen—a heart.

I'll be also the judge and the jury;
　　Step forward and learn my decree:
You must give back the heart you have stolen,
　　Or your own in return bring to me.

# "WHY DO I LOVE MY LOVE?"

### A WOMAN'S REASON.

I LOVE my love, but scarce know why  
   I love my love so true ;  
The reason must be this, that I  
   Do love—because I do.

Love has no reason, this we prove ;  
   Then pray where is the use  
To name a reason for my love ?  
   Love is love's own excuse.

Then ask me not the wherefore, pray,  
   .Love in my heart doth live,  
That heart I give, and only say,  
   I give—because I give.

The bird that builds its airy nest  
   In leafy bough on high,  
So round, so strong, so smoothly pressed  
   Knows not the reason why.

Love's like the bird that in the breast  
   May build its home, I trow,

And hovers o'er its downy nest,
　　Nor " wherefore" seeks to know.

Love is a priceless joy, I wist,
　　And love is blind, they say,
Yet none his meshes may untwist,
　　Nor break love's weave away.

Then put no price upon your love,
　　Nor reason why 'tis true ;
God's light doth shine in heaven above,
　　Because—God bids it to.

Not for my beauty, that must fade,
　　Though bright as noonday sun ;
Nor for my wit, were I a maid,
　　Would I be wooed or won.

Not for my grace nor worldly pelf,
　　Nor fame nor treasure-trove,
But love me for my very self,
　　And just because you love.

No jewels rare we prize above
　　A love that's fond and true ;
But if you love me, only love
　　Me—just because you do.

August, 1875.

# THE DEW-DROP.

I saw a diamond glistening in the grass,
Along a path where once I chanced to pass.
It blazed with changing, scintillating light ;
I knew the gem was precious, for it shone so bright.
I stood and watched its iridescent rays,
Now gold, now silver, now in purple, blaze.
Methought such beautiful, such shimmering rays of
　　　light
Could ne'er before have gladdened any mortal's sight.
I closer stepped to grasp the gem—'twas but a drop of
　　　dew,
Its glorious rays were Heaven's beams the sun sent
　　　shining through.

## RETRO ET PROSA.

THE delirium is over, the ecstasy past,
The sweet dream has vanished, 'twas too sweet to last ;
But the pleasure awakened by loving caress
Shall linger forever to comfort and bless,
For memory will treasure the bliss of the past.

Ah, joys that were brightest ! Ah, dreams that have
       fled !
Ah, visions of lost love ! Ah, hopes that are dead !
Will the future that waits for us over the main
Restore to our lives that lost Eden again ?
Will our hungering souls with love's manna be fed ?

## PLATONIC LOVE.

As plainly then so plainly now
I feel that light kiss on my brow :
  Not as one sips
  From dewy lips,
E'en though the draught should bless me ;
'Twere wrong thus to caress me,—
My lips he kissed them not.

So every time, from then till now,
We part his kiss imprints my brow ;
  He never yet
  The seal hath set
Upon my lips ; and this but proves
That well and truly, purely, loves
The one who loves and wrongs me not.

Once I forgot and lifted to his own, my lips,
As one who drinks, to cup from which he sips ;
  But he was strong,
  And said, " 'Tis wrong,"
Though lips of mine he never blessed,
Nor seal of love on them impressed ;
My lips shall bless him though he kissed them not.

I'm sure, most sure, he loves me well,
Though how I know I scarce can think or tell;
      He told me not;
      I read (perhaps) his thought.
'Twere better so, for only passion moves
The man who kneels, and vows, and swears he loves;
My love would wrong me not.

What use have we for words? The birds rejoice,
And sing of love in carols, wordless voice;
      Why plight our troth?
      Should we, when both
By intuition know what each one feels?
No honeyed words the thought conceals.
Until caressing right is his the kiss shall wrong me not.

THE joys of an ecstasy past,
 The bliss of a loving caress,
While life in the bosom doth last,
 In the heart ever lingers to bless.

A mem'ry without a regret
 Proveth real a midsummer's dream ;
Blissful moments we never forget
 As we drift on time's hastening stream.

Nature's path leadeth up to the Lord ;
 Nature's pleasures are free from alloy ;
Nature's duties will bring their reward ;
 Nature's book teaches how to enjoy.

## THE MINSTREL.

FANCY now that I'm a minstrel, only listen to my lay;
Thou shalt be my love ideal, for 'tis true, as poets say,
We must on earth love something, and I have no lover
    real ;
So, perhaps, it e'en were better that I choose a beau
    ideal.

I will clothe thee with all virtues, everything that's
    good and pure,
All the graces, highest pleasures, that ennoble and en-
    dure,
Wisdom's mantle, honor's signet, and the priceless
    pearls of truth,—
Stay time's flight and clip his pinions; give thy heart
    undying youth.

I will wreathe thy brow with laurel, and my off'ring to
    complete,
Forward bend thy crownèd forehead. See, my heart
    lies at thy feet,
And the longing in my bosom as my eager eyes uplift
Is that thou wilt prize more highly than another might,
    the gift.

True as steel is to the magnet, or the needle to the
    pole,
Is to thee my heart's allegiance; for my soul salutes thy
    soul,—
Not to every one who asketh can I yield my heart
    unto,
But to thee, who, being human, still art loving, grand,
    and true.

Asking nothing, only hoping, as my gaze dare meet
    thine eyes,
I shall see within them beaming nothing less than
    pleased surprise.
Take my treasure, proud yet tender, though it leaves
    me all alone;
Be it not as freely given, I'll not e'en accept thine
    own.

## LOVE'S SWEET PASSION.

Love's sweet passion thrills me, fills me
    With a trembling, strange desire,
Through my being flowing, glowing,
    As a bright, ecstatic fire.

Yet its light still warms me, charms me
With an ecstasy divine;
Nor its glow alarms, nor harms me.
Glad am I love's thrill is mine.

June, 1875.

--------

# UNREST.

Who has not looked forth from a bright, cheerful
room,
Looked forth into darkness, peered out in the gloom,
With a longing-filled breast,
And a nameless unrest,
While watching for one who perhaps ne'er will come?

Who thus waiting and watching in vain has not thought,
With a lingering heart-ache, he cares for me naught!
Were he swayed by my will,
His whole being should thrill,
And his footsteps should haste, by the spell I had
wrought.

November, 1874.

## LOVE'S PLEADING.

THINK of me, darling; of thee am I thinking,
  Ever and always most fondly of thee.
Drink to me, darling, the nectar I'm drinking, —
  Drink of the cup that brings sweetness to me.

Dream of me, darling; of thee am I dreaming,
  Day-time and night-time and all of the time.
Purest of pleasure is ever in seeming,
  And dreams may come true in happier clime.

Pray for me, darling; for thee am I praying,
  That all earthly blessings be showered on thee;
As from fountain refreshing, whose waters are playing,
  Thy fount or thy well-spring of joy will I be.

Love me, oh, darling! for thee am I loving,
  'Tis joy fraught with grief, and bliss thrilled with
      pain.
Tell me you love me, my love still approving.
  Ah, how can I doubt it! yet tell me again.

Cling to me, darling; to thee am I clinging;
  Be strong to sustain me, I'm only a vine,

Yet a beautiful grace and a fragrance I'm bringing,
  Ah! close round thy heart let my tendrils entwine.

Fly to me, darling; to thee am I flying,
  In spirit I come, for my spirit is thine.
Ah! list to its longing that breathes forth in sighing
  An ecstasy sweet, that is thine, love, and mine.

  March, 1875.

## THE OAK AND THE VINE.

AH, yes! I know he loves me;
I'm sure his heart approves me;
My heart with joy is thrilling;
    An ecstasy divine,
My dreams of bliss fulfilling,
    For bliss untold is mine.

His love would never grieve me,
Nor e'er on earth deceive me;
He is an oak-tree lending
    Protection to the vine,
Whose leaves with his are blending,
    Whose tendrils round him twine.

Forever will he love me,
None e'er be prized above me.

10

Around his heart I'm creeping,
  A close embrace is mine,—
The branches over-leaping
  As they to me incline.

Ah ! may his love retain me,
His strength for e'er sustain me !
For I to him am clinging
  A fragile, tender vine ;
My leaves are swaying, swinging,
  But close my tendrils twine.

For climbing, may he love me ;
For love, his heart approve me.
My heart its way is winging
  Where branch and tendrils twine,
And, nestling there, is singing
  Of joy and love divine !

June, 1875.

# LIFE.

LIFE is a toil,
Unceasing turmoil.
A hill to climb,
A rest—some time ;
A battle to fight,
To dare and do right ;
A current to brave
In the seething wave,
Or outward to glide
With the ebbing tide.
'Tis a race to be run
Till the goal is won ;
A bark on the wave
We must struggle to save ;
A hope—only this,
A semblance of bliss ;
A journey begun ;
(Would the journey were done !)
A longing for love,
Its expression above ;
A nameless unrest ;
A wish to be blest ;

A joy and a tear,
Life mingles them here ;
A tortuous road
Through a tangled wood ;
A lingering regret ;
A grief to forget ;
A ceasing from strife,
Is the ending of life.

---

## ONLY A DREAM.

ONLY a dream,
Beautiful dream,
Like the last faint ray of the sunset's gleam,—
Airiest fancy, beautiful theme,—
Shadows they are, yet so real they seem,
Brightest of visions, how real ye seem !

Over the sky
Fleecy clouds fly ;
So in our dreaming the fancies float by,
Flitting like breath of a midsummer sigh,
As love-light that beams in the glance of an eye.
Why must they vanish, oh, why ! tell me why ?

Empyrean dye,—
Azure so high,—
The glories of heaven, thy tints underlie.
It seemeth sometimes thou art coming more nigh.
Only a dream !   Thou art ever as high.
My longing may reach thee, perhaps, by and by.

Dream, faintest glint
Of sunshine, a hint
That grief on the soul will leave its imprint,
As the impress is stamped by the die of the mint.
A lingering echo, a sad, sober tint,
The impress of a shadowy hint.

The fairy-like trace
Of delicate lace,
Or beautiful landscape on window-glass ;
The net-work King Frost weaves of mimicry's grace
Will vanish as beauty fades out from a face :
So sunbeams dispel dreams as shadows they chase.

Dreaming for years,
Dreaming, though tears
Steal forth from closed eyelids ; yet sorrow endears,
As still in the mind a loved scene reappears ;
Long agone dreams the heart ever reveres :
Though they vanish, they teach us to banish our fears.

10*

Still may I dream,
Still may I deem
Thou art mine own, as in dreaming doth seem;
Though hope even fade as the sunset's last gleam,
Still in my mind airy fancies will teem,
And memory cherish the beautiful dream.

## ELDEST, RICHEST, RAREST.

Written on receipt of a letter from a friend, inclosing some lines from Shelley's unpublished poems.

AGE, 'tis true, improves the wine;
Time love's sweets can never cloy.
Richest vintage,—ripe the wine,—
So pure love without alloy,
Precious gold is from the mine,—
Priceless, purest joy.

With love's wine the heart is blest,—
Eldest, richest, rarest,—
I, with care and grief oppressed,
Prize love e'er the dearest.
Near love's fountain let me rest,—
Love, the brightest, fairest.

Man may prune the tender vine,
　　Its tendrils gain new strength ;
The heart that's pruned by hand divine
　　Bears perfect fruit at length,
For upward still its thoughts incline ;
　　Thus trained, the heart gains strength.


Flowers of love take root in earth,
　　And, though first leaves be riven,
To other tendrils putting forth
　　Greater strength is given,
Upreaching e'er, though low the birth,
　　Find perfect bloom in heaven.

---

## LOVE'S DISTRUST.

'TWAS a dream, idle praise, idle thought,
All you said, and by you soon forgot,
　　And the love of your heart
　　Is not mine.—Beauty's right,
　　God forbid I in love should delight,—
　　From my heart love depart.

## "THE SPIRIT'S EMBRACE."

My spirit greets you,
Flies to, and meets you,
Like a birdling let loose, unfettered and free.
And since it hath found you,
It hovers around you,
As the bird round its nest in the sheltering tree.

Its airy breathings,
Like smoke-cloud wreathings,
May hold you in thrall as a bright phantasy.
Does it whisper, " I love you,"
Or sway you and move you?
Thoughts I dare not utter it whispers for me.

As leaflets are swaying
When zephyrs are playing
O'er Æolian harp, waking sweet melody,
Soul-whispers above you
Are sighing, I love you,
Thus ecstasy's longing I'm breathing o'er thee.

Sweet visions of beauty,
Of love, and of duty,
Our spirits are taught by the spirit above;

Pure as snow-flakes, which, meeting,
Their mission completing,
Dissolve, not in tears, but in essence of love.


Is it but seeming?
Am I but dreaming
Thy spirit and mine now are meeting in space?
The charm let us break not,
Dream on and awake not,—
God blesses the union when spirits embrace.

March 8, 1875.

---

## I COME TO LOVE THEE.

I COME in spirit, and I hover near thee;
Thy longing for a presence still to cheer thee
Doth henceforth evermore to me endear thee,
I come to love thee.


And ere I come and lowly bow before thee
Thou seest, love, and knowest I adore thee,
E'en when thou art afar, in spirit bending o'er thee,
I come to love thee.

Thus loving, I love dearly to caress thee,
Close to my throbbing heart I love to press thee,
To breathe sweet incense o'er thee that may bless thee,
       I come to love thee.

What though thy languid blood is fast congealing?
Thy heart shall wake to richer, warmer feeling,
For I come warmest, deepest love revealing,
       I come to love thee.

Thy spirit through thy verse breathed forth a longing,
That claimed my inner self as to itself belonging,
And thus commingling loving thoughts came thronging,
       I come to love thee.

Wisdom and age but make me more revere thee,
Thy kindly goodness doth the more endear thee,
Thy love doth make it Eden to be near thee,
       I come to love thee.

# BOTANY.

VIOLETS, sweet violets,
I love you as I love my pets.
Let me see,—
One, two, three,
Four, five,—ever five leaves;
Always the same,—never deceives.
What care I for your family?
What did you say?
Botany?
Fling it in Botany Bay.

Daisies, daisies,
Scattered in endless mazes
Over the meadows, under the hedges,
Not in the path, but close to its edges;
As stars gem the blue of the sky with their sheen,
Ye gem and besprinkle the velvety green.
What care I for your pedigree?
Pistils or stamens, how many there be!
What did you say?
Botany?
Fling it in Botany Bay.

Buttercup !
Hey, johnny-jump-up !
Johnny will tell if I pull you apart,—
If I pick you to pieces and tear out your heart,
Johnny will tell,
I know him well,
So keep your heart in its golden bell.
What care I how rich it be !
I love you, and that is enough for me.
What did you say ?
Botany ?
Fling it in Botany Bay.

Forget-me-not !
I love the spot
Where grows the fairy forget-me-not.
How like to a star
Its pale blossoms are !
And its bonny bright eyes I love to see.
What care I how many there be ?
What did you say ?
Botany ?
Fling it in Botany Bay.

Mignonnette !
I'll never forget
Thy fragrance, it lingers about me yet.

Delicate blossom,
Rest on my bosom;
Shed a sweet incense, when dying, o'er me,—
When no longer thy fairy-like blossoms I'll see.
What did you say?
Botany?
Fling it in Botany Bay.

Lily so fair!
Purity's there.
You have beautiful raiment and never a care.
Oh, would I might be
So lovely as thee,
And have never a thought about "nothing to wear!"
I'd belong to your "tribe," whatever it be.
What did you say?
Botany?
Fling it in Botany Bay.

Cowslips!
Dewy lips,
Thy name recalls bright childhood scenes;
For thy blossoms I look,
In the mead by the brook,
Through the vista of time that intervenes;
Again I chase the wingèd hours
And gather thy yellow unfolding flowers,
Golden boats all afloat on a green leafy sea.

What did you say?
Botany?
Fling it in Botany Bay.

Bluebells, bluebells,
What have you hid in your airy cells?
Azure of heaven,
Dewdrops of even,—
Whisper, bluebells, whisper to me,
I only know how fair you be,
Without a thought of your family.
What did you say?
Botany?
Fling it in Botany Bay.

Fair budding rose,—
I may not close
Without a tribute in verse to thee.
" First love !"
May it prove
Source of joy like flowers to me,
Whatever their names or their family.
What did you say?
Botany?
Fling it in Botany Bay.

Orange blossom !
Adorning the bosom,
Or twined in the curl of a fair lady's hair ;

Ah, sometimes you be
But a mockery;
Her lips may be false, though her brow seem so fair,—
Then so many heart-aches you blossoms are.
Joy, trouble, or care is your progeny,
A various, wonderful family.
What did you say?
Botany?
Fling it in Botany Bay.


Pansies are fraught
With beautiful thought;
Bright thought and golden, and brilliant in hue;
Give me the blue one, that is the true one.
I'll have nothing to do—
Pansy, would you?—
With " genus," or " classes," or " family."
You bring a thought, a dear thought to me.
A thought, did I say?
For my botany?
No, fling it in Botany Bay.


Poppy—nepenthe—
Tell me who sent thee
To lull me to sleep o'er my botany?
So drowsy am I—
I cannot tell why—

Nor how—many—stamens—or—poppies I see,
When I wake I'll remember how many there be.
What did you say?
Botany?
Go fling it in Botany Bay.

## PEARLS OF THOUGHT.

WITH head low bowed, and eyelids heavy laden
    With grief and sorrow and fast-falling tears,
I, tired and footsore, seeking distant Aidenn,
    Am wandering through the path of weary, troubled
        years.
The way is rough, the clouds are black around me,
    Temptation's dragon still besets my path;
Trials and dangers, like the clouds, surround me,
    And smother, like the deadly simoon's breath.
An arid desert I have crossed, affliction.
    Experience, my guide, has led me by the hand,
His lamp he loaned me; by its faint reflection
    I found some thought-pearls on the desert sand;
And some were clear and delicate in tinting,
    And over some a darker shade was cast,

As though by fire seared, whose scorch had left imprint-
    ing,
  Or fiery breath had dimmed them as it passed.
But over all I found some hope-rays shining,
  Which gave new beauty to each added gem,
And roused me from my sorrowing, sad repining,
  To weave the pearls of thought into a diadem.
The many gems I gathered patiently I sought,
  Until, well-laden, from the blinding sands I rose,
And, lifting up to heaven's light my pearls of thought,
  Behold, each one thereafter fairer, brighter grows.
Not mine the thoughtless, joyous, happy ringing
  Of careless glee, or gayety and mirth;
Ever in low, sad tones my brooding heart is singing,—
  Like wounded bird I sing, and hover near the earth.
Had I not walked through suffering and sadness,
  The pearly gems that beam with light divine
I ne'er had gathered,—gems of chastened gladness,—
  Nor would the priceless treasure, thought, been mine.
I sowed the tears, they were the overflowing
  Of deep emotion from my stricken heart ;
But I could ne'er believe till now the sowing
  Would richest harvest, purest joy, impart.
Whence come these pearly gems ?  What brought them
  To mingle in the desert's sandy waste ?
Ah, many another fruitlessly hath sought them,—
  The pearls of thought which in the diadem are placed,

They grow not in the garden of fruition;
   For hope fulfilled ne'er gave a thought-pearl birth.
Though wealth may seek, or fame, or high position,
    Their price is tears, a stricken heart, a head low-
       bowed to earth.
The wounded bivalve in the depth of ocean
   May from that wound a pearly gem bring forth:
So hearts when pierced and trembling with emotion
   To pearly, priceless gems of thought give birth.
One way we have, one only way of knowing,
   How bitter drops when spilled from the full cup,—
Through nights of grief the tears to pearly gems are
     growing,
   They are the seed from which pure pearls spring up.
If I at length shall reach a green oasis
   In desert life, whose fount may cheer and bless
My thirsting heart, I'll lift a song of praises,
   And thread my pearls, erst tears of bitterness.

   March, 1875.

# REUNION.

Once more again, brave soldiers, stand,
A scarworn, maimed, and veteran band,
Grasping in fellowship each hand,
By link uniting all this land,—
A link inured by battles dared,
More firmly joined by dangers shared.

Though years have flown full half a score
Since clasped these hands in days of yore,
Call back those years, retread once more
Those battle-fields, those days live o'er
Which memories to the mind restore,
Casting aside Time's misty screen,
Painting anew each thrilling scene,
O'er hill and gulch or deep ravine.

Recount once more the havoc done
When Indiana's stalwart son,
When Hoosier lads went marching on,
With shot and shell and booming gun;
How starry eve or morning sun
More brightly shone on battles won;

How, Union colors planted here,
Ye rent the air with many a cheer.

That banner, then so proudly borne,
Shall never be of glory shorn,
Though faded, old, and sadly torn,—
Symbol of veterans scarred and worn,—
That veteran flag so proudly borne,
Leading you on with drum and fife
To save your country with your life.

That flag o'er this fair land must wave
Till nations sleep in freedom's grave ;
That emblem led the true and brave,
And countless thousands freely gave
Their lives its starry folds to save,
Who conquered armed tyranny
That millions more might still be free.

And, oh ! forget not, pray you tell
How thirty thousands—name them well—
For freedom fought and bravely fell,
Languished and died in prison-cell,
Lie sleeping now in plain or dell,
Who answer not from field or plain,
Whose footsteps ne'er return again !

My thoughts keep guard with funeral tread
O'er silent bivouac of the dead,
O'er fields where friends and foes have bled,
O'er hospital or prison-bed,
O'er plains where death his phalanx led.
My mind is as a lettered tome
In which is writ, " They ne'er came home."

Yet memory brings them back to me,
Who answer not the reveille,
Whose loving smiles I ne'er shall see,
Whose voice hear not—must ever be
Cherished, preserved by memory.
Their names enshrined in history,
Till trumpet-sound, on that great day,
Shall gather all who marched away.

Greater than he who wears a crown,
Or purple robe or ermined gown,
Greater than he who wins renown,
Who with his arms his life lays down ;
Ay, memory's torchlight brightly burns
For him who never more returns.

Ah ! many hearts are sad and lone,
Whose grieved refrain an echoing tone

Like muffled drum hides stifled moan
That else would be a throbbing groan.
Glory to them, each one and all,
Who answered to the nation's call!
Joy—you who meet, all battles o'er,—
I, weeping, wail—returned no more!

---

# ECHO RIVER.

### IN MAMMOTH CAVE, KENTUCKY.

SUNBEAMS never, mystic river,
Nor the moonbeams, o'er thee quiver;
Not the faintest starlight gleam
Shines above thee, sombre stream.
Night-enshrouded river Echo,
Mournful dirge so sadly slow,
Loudly clear or soft and low,
Singing as we gliding go,—
O'er thy waters' silent flow
Comes the echo—"Lo."
See the shimmering shadows playing,
Born of torchlights' fitful swaying,
Cast upon the cavern wall,
Cast o'er Echo River Hall,

Hear the echo call,
Answering echo—" All."

And the boatman, standing grimly,
Throws a shadow weird, unseemly,
On the rocky space,
Strangely out of place,
As it were a network ghostly—"Lace."
Bright winged birds have never flown
O'er thy waters dim and lone;
Shores of earth with flowers o'ergrown,
Mossy banks, lo, thou hast none;
Only walls of solid stone,
By the great Creator hewn,
By his power alone
Round thy waters—" Lone."

Wavering shadows weirdly falling,
Seem as spirits beckoning, calling,
Calling through the echo voices.
Strangely awed, our soul rejoices,
As 'twere voice from heaven calls us,
Heavenly majesty enthralls us.

Now from dome and wall surrounding,
'Gainst the massive rock resounding,

Hear the echo
Come and go.
Long we gaze in silent wonder.
We of earth—thou'rt gliding under,
Through the rock reft wide asunder.

O'er thy watery depth rock-girten
Plays the flickering light uncertain ;
　　See o'er dome and cavern hall
Tracery of mystic scroll,
" God's handwriting on the wall,"
　　All His work, His—" All."

Hearken, now the voices singing,
All the echoes backward bringing,
As a grand triumphal ringing.
Every sense with rapture filling,
Like a thousand harpstrings thrilling,
Every breath to silence stilling,
Joy divine is o'er me stealing,
　　And a bliss profound
　　Echo tells me—" Found,"
　　In the echo sound.

Long the sweet refrain will linger,
As the trace of fairy finger,

Rising now in fuller volume,
Answering from each arch and column,
Joyous peals of music ringing,
As it were the angels singing.
Loud, resonant, rising higher,
Melody of heavenly choir;
   Is it this I hear?
   Say, is heaven near?
   This the spirit sphere?
   List the echo—" Fear."


To my mind this truth is plain:
Know I now by this refrain
Words that die will live again.
And the grand resurgence rolling,
All my inner soul controlling,
   Echoes ever
   O'er the river,
Stirs this thought within my brain,
As a loudly-echoing strain,
Words may die yet live again.


Fairy river, gliding, going,
Through the cavern, winding, flowing,
To the wondrous realm beyond;
Here my thirsting soul hath found,

Peace my longing soul had wanted,
Quelled the doubts of spirit-haunted ;
Thou hast taught me more than sages,
By thy rocky clefts of ages,
Taught me more than storied pages,
Led me to the opening portal,
Proved the soul is e'er immortal ;
Brought of knowledge mighty store,
Hidden in mysterious lore.

Echoing thoughts my brain are stirring,
E'er unto my mind recurring,
Evermore this truth averring,
Thou hast taught by sure refrain,
Echoing dying words so plain,
I shall die, yet live again ;
Dying be my—" Gain."

# CLOUDS OF LIFE AND SKY.

HIDING the light, dim shadows lie;
These at approach of others fly,—
Great hills of vapor intervene
To hide the moonlight's silvery sheen.

Winged shadows flit athwart the sky,—
So clouds between my life and I
Gather and flit, or linger yet,
Faint shadows of a vague regret.

Midsummer clouds o'er sunset sky,
Like changing years, go swiftly by;
Again uniting, darkly roll,
Thus storms of grief sweep o'er the soul.

The lightest clouds that fleck the sky
May grow still lighter by and by;
If, gathering fast, they bring the rain,
Ye know the sun will shine again.

Through rifted rocks the light descry:
The star that guides our hopes on high.
The darkest night must pass away,
And after dawn comes perfect day.

When darkest cloudage dims the sky,
Look far beyond with faith's clear eye.
The storm will make the air more pure,
Life's sorrows teach us to endure.

## MEMORY.

SHE sits in the shade of a darkened room,
Surrounded by warp and woof of the loom,
And she weaves, with a wonderful magical art,
Bright pictures of happiness, dreams of the heart.
The thoughts in her mind that rise and swell,
The visions of beauty that with her dwell;
She's a beautiful being—fond, truthful, and pure,
And her fabric as lasting as life will endure.
Ah! I feel to-night all of witchery's spell,
That steals over those who with memory dwell.

In a low, sweet voice she softly trills ;
To its musical rhythm our being thrills.
O'er our senses they linger, the ebb and flow
Of the waves of the beautiful " long ago."
Ah! the sacredest chamber in every heart
Is e'er for memory set apart.

She recalls to our mind, while she weaving sings,
The long-ago pleasures that memory brings.
Should we shut her out from her place in the heart,
She keeps knocking for entrance and will not depart;
Her angelic presence of beauty and truth
Is a solace to age and a pleasure to youth.


For she gives back the long-ago days that had fled,
And the paths where our youthful feet hastened to
　　tread ;
The scenes that were brightest, the things that were
　　dear,
In a beautiful pattern she's weaving them here.
With her I oft linger, as one in a dream,
O'er the things that have been, but now only seem ;
And I yearningly gaze, as with memory I come,
On the web-woven pictures, the fruit of her loom,
As she lifteth the ideal fabric to view,—
'Tis the scenes of our past, ah, how lifelike and true !


She has woven a sad, soft sunshine and shade
In the wonderful texture her fingers have made,—
Just here a bright pattern, a sunbeam and flowers,
Recalling a vision of childhood's bright hours ;
And a golden web she faithfully weaves
Of a joyous youth, with a border of leaves,

And the sunniest days, full of childhood's glee
And youth's brightest hours, she pictures for me;
And I seem to stroll in reveries sweet
Through the path where the o'erhanging branches
    meet.

All the past returns, and the present recedes,
And I gather the flowers that sprinkle the meads:
The flowers of hope in profusion lie there,
Intertwined with the garland of love bright and fair;
Yet hope's flowers sometimes lie scattered and dead,
And the weed of despair here grows rankly instead.
Many pictures are hanging on memory's wall,
And the mist of time ever veils them all,
And the ones that rare beauties the fairest unfold
Are woven of memory's threadings of gold;
Their frames are of fanciful texture wove,—
Of the flowers of beauty, of hope, and of love.

And quickly as ever before them I pass,
She covers each picture with magical glass;
'Tis a mirror reflecting, and backward it brings
The long-vanished years on their swift-flying wings;
They are wingèd mile-posts, and each passing year
Was marked with a sorrow, a smile, or a tear;
Memory lifteth her voice, and sweetly she'll sing
Of dear forms and faces she only can bring;

Then she turns to her loom, and, weaving anew,
Bright forms and loved faces she brings to our view.

Here's a handful of flowers her fingers have wrought,
That grew in the beautiful garden of thought,
With the thread of a dream the garland is twined,
And we linger again by her power o'er the mind;
By the spell which her magic hath over us cast,
We review with memory the scenes of the past,
While she sings "long ago" to a thought beating
        time,
And measures the width by the poet's rhyme;
Then she toucheth our heart-strings, and maketh them
        thrill
By the magical grace of her own sweet will;
Then she reacheth our mind, and she bids us awake
From the lethargic sleep that our senses would take;
She leadeth us down to the work she hath wrought,
The long-vanished scenes that her genius hath caught.

What she reads in the book of our life is portrayed
With the woof and the warp, and the light and the
        shade;
Thoughts and feelings as well, and the passage of time,
Are inclosed in a mystical border of rhyme;
The pain and the anguish of by-gone years,
She weaves them all in with sorrow and tears.

Here's a sombre tint for the deserts we've crossed,
And great waves of grief where our soul hath been
          tossed ;
Here's a fairy barge with hope's promises decked,
And the gulf of despair where the vessel was wrecked.
Now a grassy green mound she pictures here,
For the loved and the lost are to memory dear.

Now her shuttle she fills with a deeper dye,
And she weaves in the glance of a bonny bright eye,
Or a sunny curl, or a dimpled cheek,
Or a pensive smile, so winning and meek ;
And again she weaves, with a golden thread,
The brightest hopes that for ever have fled.

As a sweet, sad thought comes with echo's refrain,
Thus a rapturous thrill memory gives us again.
Oh, how dear is her presence, who, sitting apart,
Still lingers to bless us in depth of our heart !
Her form hath a magic and nameless grace,
And she rules us, a queen in her God-given place.

Thought and truth twined the garland enwreathing her
          brow.
Ah ! she reaches my mind : she is swaying it now ;
She causeth the color to come and go
On the cheek, like the ceaseless ebb and flow

Of the waves on the beach or the pebbly strand,
Embracing, receding, and kissing the land.
Those who dwell with memory shall see and know
And recall the sweet visions of long, long ago;
And the fabrical scroll by memory unfurled
Brings the visions and joys of a long-agone world.

But glance through her glass at her pictures, and see
The sweet thoughts and sad ones she bringeth to thee,
And yield to the spell which she casteth o'er me,—
Yea, blessed forever shall memory be!

## THE CULPRIT.

Guilty of loving? I fear it is true,
If to think is a crime, for I *think* I love you;
For I tremble with joy when I know you are near,
And your voice sends a thrill through my being, my
    dear.

Say, thinkest thou not, like a simpleton, elf,
I am bringing the proof that convicts but myself?
Yet, "honor 'mong thieves," I the secret impart
To you as a thief, for you've stolen—my heart.

Love comes when he will, goes without being sent,
And I've surely committed no wrong with intent;
And I hope, as 'twas done without malice prepense,
You'll forgive, if you can, my first loving offense.

## THE MASK.

I HAVE walked 'midst the tumult and glare all day,
With a grim-faced duty I must obey;
Who, when I would wander, still bids me to stay,
Though I fain would hide me from all away;
And I yearn from my soul with care so oppressed,
I long for happiness, quiet, and rest.

But I hide my heart 'neath a mask of steel,
I stifle its moan and its wailing conceal,
That no idle hand its deep throbbing may feel,
Displacing the mask, all its longing reveal.
But oft in the darkness, when daylight has flown,
I commune with my sorrow when sitting alone.

# CHARITY.

DEDICATED TO THE LADIES' RELIEF SOCIETY, DECEMBER 9, 1875.

SHE's a friend indeed, a friend in need ;
She hath no lengthened and tiresome screed,
But kindness in word and thought and deed
Is what she teacheth,—the only creed
      Of Charity.

She giveth good words that ever are fraught
With priceless treasures of kindly thought ;
Thus laden with comfort that cannot be bought
Are the cheering words that ever are brought
      By Charity.

She healeth the wounded hearts that bleed ;
She heareth the yearning of hearts that plead ;
She answers with generous act and deed,
And hastens the hungering ones to feed,
      Doth Charity.

She helpeth the faltering step to sustain ;
She bringeth a solace for care and pain ;

She forgiveth a wrong yet again and again,
She harbors no malice : that cannot remain
      With Charity.

Another's misfortune she'll deplore ;
She refuseth her mercy to none who implore ;
She turneth no wanderer from her door ;
She gives what she can, with a will to give more,
      Doth Charity.

She for wretched and outcast doth sympathy feel ;
By dying bedside doth praying kneel ;
The record of errors she will not reveal,
But close it with silence,—the tender seal
      Of Charity.

Encouraging words most kindly to speak,
To shelter God's lambs from the winds so bleak,
To help the needy, protect the weak,
Ay, this is the mission, if mission you seek,
      Of Charity.

The naked are clothed, the hungry are fed,
And ministers sent to the dying bed,
And, when the life-light for ever hath fled,
Then tenderly closed are the eyes of the dead
      By Charity.

She upholdeth the feeble lest they shall fall,
She never neglecteth the sufferer's call,
She entereth hovels where woe doth appall
The bravest heart, for greatest of all
　　　Is Charity.

Her platform is broad, her precepts will win,
She teacheth that all in the world are akin;
Her religion will take all humanity in;
A mantle that covers a mountain of sin
　　　Hath Charity.

And, oh! remember, the Scriptures say
That "With you the poor ye have alway;"
Then heed the call of the poor, I pray,
And minister to them from day to day
　　　With Charity.

Contribute your mite, do the good ye can do,
It will bring you a joy both lasting and new;
With generous hand aid the noble few,—
These women who labor with impulse true
　　　For Charity.

Your giving shall be your goodliest gain;
" Cast your bread on the waters," it will sustain

Some sinking life, and return again
From grateful hearts you have saved from pain
　　　By Charity.


Ay, blessed shall be the unwearying feet
That stay not their steps for the rain or sleet,
But haste the demands of hunger to meet;
They shall find a rest and recompense sweet
　　　Through Charity.


And blessed are they who ever will find
In their thoughts a kindness for all mankind,
For this is the brotherly tie that doth bind,
Whoso loveth the Lord, and whose hearts are inclined
　　　To Charity.


Then bring to her temple no meagre dole,
And the angel above shall your names enroll
In letters of gold on a mystic scroll;
She strengthens the body and saveth the soul,
　　　Doth Charity.


Let generous thoughts and actions accord.
Who gives to the needy but lends to the Lord;
Who lendeth to Him shall receive a reward
　　　For Charity.

## TO MYLA.

### ON HER TENTH BIRTHDAY.

LITTLE daughter, precious child,
Lift thy soulful eyes so mild,
While I tell thee what I bring
For a birthday offering.

Prize it, then, all else above,
Priceless gift is mother-love,
Shielding thee from care and strife;
Mother loves thee more than life.

Ten winged years have o'er thee flown,
Soon thou'lt be to woman grown;
Years are leaves that, one by one
The rose unfolds, till fully blown.

Silent prayers for thee I breathe,
Hope's fair flowers for thee I wreathe;
Prayers and hopes, from day to day,
Send I forth to guard thy way.

Be thou ever pure and fair
As unfolding rosebuds are;

Scatter kindness, e'en as they
Shed a fragrance o'er the way.

May good deeds, from opening morn
Till its close, thy life adorn;
Be thou fresh and sweet and true,
A flower baptized in heaven's dew.

Myla came but yesterday
Pleading to me from her play;
And, "Mamma, I wish," said she,
"You would write a verse for me."

Could I then that wish refuse?
Called I to my aid the muse;
Bring I, darling, now with this
Mother-love and birthday kiss.

# IS IT LOVE?

So, you cannot help but love me,
　　Prythee tell me why;
Soon you'll praise some one above me,
　　Love for me will die.

But I know not that you love me;
　　How can I believe?
Nay, I know not how to prove thee,
　　Men will so deceive.

Thank you kindly, as you say so,
　　For the love you bring,
Only fearing that love may so
　　Very soon take wing.

Love is fickle as a shadow,
　　Flitting here and there,
Over brook, or wood, or meadow,
　　Flitting everywhere.

If you cannot help but love me,
　　Then I must forgive;
Though I even must reprove thee
　　That you let love live.

13*

And you say I'm very sweet, sir;
  How, sir, do you know?
And indeed it is not meet, sir,
  That you tell me so.


And you say that all the sweetness
  Of a hundred more
Do but form the full completeness
  Of my honeyed store.


Ah, I fear you would deceive, sir,
  Feeding me with chaff;
Unbelieving still I grieve, sir,
  Doubtingly I laugh.


And you call me very good, sir;
  Hope I this is true;
And I'm very sure you should, sir,
  Try to be good, too.


But with me, ah! much I fear, sir,
  Loving days are o'er;
If you love me half a year, sir,
  I shall prize love more.


And the feeling, rightly name it,
  Is it love alone?

Let no baser passion claim it
    For its very own.

Love me truly, fondly, dearly,
    Let your love ne'er fall ;
If you do not love sincerely,
    Love me not at all.

## DAISIES AND BUTTERCUPS.

Daisies and buttercups, lovely are ye,
Daisies and buttercups, seeming to be
Drifting and swaying on meadowy sea,
Nodding and bending and bowing to me,
Ye wave o'er the billowy, flowery lea.

A golden cup and a porcelain plate,
With gold embossed,—I shall banquet in state
From fairy flowers that zephyrs undate ;
I will dine with love, I will banish hate,
And the nectar of gods my mind shall elate.

This flowery censer with gold enwrought,
With costliest, rarest of dainties is fraught,

And laden with clusters of beautiful thought;
I gather their sweets which nepenthe hath brought,
For which my sad mind had long languishing sought.

As the shimmering waves around me roll,
I partake, as I rest on a billowy knoll,
Of feast of reason and flow of soul;
'Tis a mystic chalice, thy golden bowl,
And I quaff from its hollow no meagre dole.

As I lift the goblet filled to the brink,
Encorraled about with a green leafy link,
The bright cups jingle, and seem to clink
With a joyous ring as I stoop to drink,
And, wrapped in day-dreams, I blissfully sink;

And a purer thrill of pleasure is mine
Than any that lurks in the sparkling wine
From the purple wealth of the leafy vine.
This richest surfeit can never be thine
Till thou drinkest to love and kneel at love's shrine.

There's a mystical spell in the goblet, I ween,
That giveth new beauty to velvety green,
That addeth a glory to shimmering sheen
Cast over the waves gliding through the ravine,
For a golden halo encircles each scene.

There's a cloud-capped mountain that loometh high
Through the ethery blue of a tropical sky,
Where the kisses of muses float airily by,
Borne on the breath of a zephyr's soft sigh,
And I yearningly longed to its summit to fly.

Far up, where the clouds and the mountain greet,
There's a fountain pure and as nectarine sweet,
Whose waters e'er flow with a rhythmical beat;
Here it is that the naiads and muses meet,
And quaff from this fountain of bliss complete.

That I never could reach this fountain I knew,
Yet my longing took wings and heavenward flew,
Through the vasty depth of empyrean blue,
To the waters which, tasted, none ever may rue,
Then whispered my thought to Thalia so true.

As I drink to love, and love drinketh to me,
From the flower-cup sweets, as culls honey the bee;
O'er thy swaying bloom, like a sigh o'er the sea,
'Tis the muses that murmur. Thalia gave me
To sip from the fountain of Castaly.

For the gentle muse, with a sympathy true,
Leaning over the marge where fair flowers grew,

Caught the drips from the fountain and upward threw;
As she flung them aloft, they descended in *dew*,
And fell in the cup, love, I'm drinking to you.

Still over the meadow the zephyrs that blow
Are whispering ever in breathings low,
That thrill me with pleasure.   With joy I glow,
And an ecstatic thrill through my being doth flow,
Yet the source of my pleasure I scarcely may know.

Oh, daisies and buttercups! never I see
Thy swaying bloom but there cometh to me
Fancies recurring and fancies that flee,
And I yearningly long for quiet with thee:
From the world and its tumult I long to be free.

# AN ADDRESS

### TO THE BODY OF A MAN IN THE WHIRLPOOL—NIAGARA.

Ah, how ceaseless the rounds which, in darkness and
      gloom,
Thou hast made in the noisy confines of thy tomb!
    Since the whirlpool so great,
    Like a maelstrom of fate,
    Did surround thee, ay, drowned thee,
    None heard thee; it stirred thee
    And whirled thee to death.
Rising up, sinking down, with a thundering sound,
Thou art lashed by its fury around and around.
    Now to sight you are lost;
    Like a bubble you're tossed
    By the torrent's strong clasp,
    By the raging wave's grasp,
    Around and around,
    Whilst the thundering sound
    Rings still on deaf ears,
    As it did ere you drowned.
Ah! who were thy friends who mourn thy sad fate?
How many are made, by thy death, desolate?

These questions we ask, yet we never shall know
Who was tossed by these waters, now high and now
      low;
    Now fast and now slow,
As the wild gleaming whirlpool compels thee t
      go;
    Now a hand or a foot,
    (Incased in a boot,)
    Or a glimpse of a face;
But quickly 't has vanished,—too quickly to trace
Out its features.  Oh, terrible jest!
'Tis said, after death, that the body finds rest,—
Finds rest.  Seest thou thine?  It is whirling about
From the seething caldron; 'twill never get out.
Didst fancy a fate like to this,—that thou must
Be beaten and pounded and hastened to dust,
    With a din and a roar
    Like the cannon's outpour?
    Didst thou ever think,
    As thou stoodst on the brink
And looked on the rapids, that when thou wer
      dead
They should grind thee to dust for Niagara's bed?
Nor will it be long ere the eddying throng—
Waves we read of in story and picture in song—
Will dash thee to pieces with shriek and with groan;
For e'en droppings of water will wear away stone,

Will rend thy limp limbs, and will tear them apart,
Will reach to thy vitals and pluck out thy heart,
 Till no one can see
 What resemblance there be
Of one who was once a poor mortal like me !

## CHRISTMAS DREAMS.

Night before Christmas, you bear on your wing
 Fancies so bright and hopes full of joy ;
Like chiming carols they merrily ring .
 From cherry-red lips of each girl and boy,
"I wonder what 'Santa' will bring?"

Beautiful eyes now are hidden from sight,
 'Neath fringed white lids that over them close ;
Sunny curls fall with a softening light
 Over the pillow where sweetly repose
Our little ones pure and bright.

For Myla and Nattie are fast asleep ;
 They watched for "Santa" long as they could,
But, so sleepy, at last to bed they creep,
 While Myla said, "Tell him bring somsin dood."
Now, angels, your watch o'er them keep.

They sleep, and visions of dolly or drum,
   Like vapors, are floating airily by;
Visions of trumpet and great sugar-plum
   Are seeming all night before them to fly,
Fairy fancies that go and come.


They wake.   List the words of gleeful surprise:
   "When we sleeped, then old Santa did tum!"
"And binged," said Myla, "a dolly yat ties!"—
   "And see," says Nattie, "my sled, and a drum"—
"An' my baby tan shuts its yies.


"And nuts and tandy, and everysing,
   He binged me 'em all," said little pet.
"Dess fits my finer 'is ittie dold ying.
   I wos 'faid old Santa 'Taus would fordet,
Cos so many he had to bing."


And sturdy Nat to his dear mother flew:
   "Just see my book and a nice new hat,
And mittens, and boots, and a French harp, too!
   So much I did wish he would bring me that!
But I wonder how Santa knew?"


Vision of childhood, so joyous and sweet,
   Happiest hours when life is new;

As the Christmas dawn you hopefully greet,
    May ever your brightest of dreams come true,
Your joy, your bliss to complete!

Beautiful eyes, may you waken to joy,
    And the Christ-child bless each humble home!
To each household pet, or motherless boy,
    May Santa Claus never forget to come,
Bringing pleasures without alloy!

---

## DOUBT NOT.

'Tis he of little faith
    Who, when the sunshine glows
And flowers adorn his path,
    With fickle thought a doubt bestows
For all the good he hath.

How painful, yet how sweet
    Is love and doubt and joy!
The rose is incomplete
    Without its thorn; without alloy
No bliss on earth we meet.

Yet woman's trusting love
 Is true and sweet and sure,
Nestling like Heaven's own dove,
 As fair and as divinely pure,
Descending from above.

Richest who giveth most,
 Asking for no return.
Ay, this shall be love's boast,
 Who loveth most its truth may learn,
Truth proved by loving host.

Perchance a pleased surprise,
 Though I may not behold,
Beameth within your eyes,
 Seemeth, as I my thoughts unfold,
I, too, before you rise.

Love's ties are those that bind,
 For love will claim his own,
Though love unwisely blind,
 With sorrow must for bliss atone,
Yet keeps his idol shrined.

Never with doubt nor fear
 Distrust a love so fair,
Breathing its message dear,
 " Oh, darling ! I would I were there !"
Or, " Would, love, you were here !"

## M O N O D Y.

HE is dead !   He is dead !
Ah ! the words sink like lead,
   With a dull, heavy thud,
Far down in the heart's deepest well ;
'Tis the funeral knell
Of fond hopes.   Who can tell
What an anguish profound
Ever comes, sorrow-crowned,
To the heart and the brain
Which re-echo again
   The words, He is dead ! he is dead !

With a lingering refrain
Of the deepest and saddest pain,
   Re-echo the words, He is dead ;
And the heart is so weighted,
With heavy grief freighted,
That it cannot rebound
From its burden of sorrow profound.
Hark ! the funeral knell
In the tones of the bell ;
Waves of sound, how they swell !

14*

How they rise, how they roll,
Like despair o'er the soul !

He is dead !   He is dead !
His spirit hath fled,
    'Twas this that the tolling bell said.
The requiem it sings
In my mind ever rings,
To my sad soul it brings
    The words and the thought, He is dead !
And the slow tolling bell and the funeral tread
Keep time to the words, He is dead ;
Beating time, beating time to the poet's sad rhyme,
On my muffled heart they beat time.

And a shade is over my lamp of light,
The eyelids of grief still press down o'er my sight,
And a cloud of sadness surrounds my life,
Which the joys of the world nor its tumult nor strife,
Nay, naught on earth can dispel
The gloom and shadow in which I dwell.
It came with the words of the tolling bell,
And holds me in thrall like a spell.

# STRAY LEAVES.

### LOVE'S GIFT.

IF I, like love, the clouds might rift
  O'er poesy's hidden shrine,
I'd kneel in her presence, her veil uplift.
  Ah ! henceforth forever she's mine,
    She is mine!
  Henceforth and forever she's mine !

For poesy ever is love's purest gift,
    Precious gift ;
And yet, like these lines, she is thine ;
And still, like myself, she is thine,—
Love's gift, truly thine.

### II.

DID ever one love thee more truly,
More sweetly, more fondly, more fully,
  With self-abnegation complete ?

A pearl from the depth of the ocean,
A heart that e'er throbs with emotion,
  Is the gift that I lay at thy feet.


### III.

O man, O life of brief-encircled span,
Afar or near upon life's desert plain,
Thy lot, thy sphere, is only as a single grain,—
Perchance of sand, perchance of wheat,—
  Strewn on this earthly field.
The one a barren nothingness,
  The other fruit may yield.


### IV.

By the light of experience we gather
  The truths we had doubted for years,
That the rippling streamlet of laughter
  Finds its source in the fountain of tears.


### V.

In the river of life the tear-drops of woe
  Make purer the fountain, more limpid its flow.
Sorrow cleanseth the heart, refresheth like dew,
  Clears the fountain of thought as air blended in snow.

## VI.

### FRIENDS.

WHEN discouraged I am, then there come words of
    cheer,
That fall like sweet melody's chime on my ear,
From above words of comfort that help me at length,
"Though great is thy burden, yet so be thy strength."
Thank God for the blessing, the strength that He sends,
In the persons of true-hearted, brave, loving friends!

## VII.

WERE love but a mythical, fanciful theme,
But a flickering sunbeam of golden gleam,
But the mystical fount of a shadowy stream,
A vanishing vision, a beautiful dream,
How, then, could love crown us with bliss so supreme?

## VIII.

### A PRAYER.

Reply to a friend who wrote, "May God give you brain to think,
heart to feel, wings to soar, and voice to sing!"

YES, pray God give me "brain to think,"
At wisdom's fountain let me drink.
Pray God to give me "heart to feel,"
And on that heart impress His seal;

To purer air on " wings to soar,"
Until I reach the heavenly shore.
Pray, too, He give me "voice to sing,"
To voiceless love expression bring.


IX.

As the years of thy life all unheeded fly past,
May these wingèd mile-posts, e'en to the last,
Be numbered with joys all unshaded with care,
And each passing year be more bright and more fair!

May sweet evergreen memories cling round thy heart,
Buds of promise and love of life's wreath form a part,
With kind thoughts intertwined, is the wish I may bring,
And a Hawthorn (Hope's blossom) my verse offering.

# SOME DAY.

WHISPER in accents low,
    Some day,
    Gladly,
Thou lovest me more than aught below ;
    Some day,
When ruddy cheek hath lost its glow,
    And I am old,
    Thy strong arms then around me fold,
Loving me then as now.
Oh, darling ! love me so.

When I am lying low,
    Some day ;
    Sadly,
Then, thou shalt surely know,
    Some day,
My life doth outward flow,
    Like ebbing tide ;
    Sit, then, my dying couch beside,
Smoothing my fevered brow ;
I shall more quiet grow.

When painful angry throe,
        Some day,
        Madly
Chaseth my life-blood till it cease to flow ;
        Some day,
When aching heart shall throb so slow,
        My wasted cheek
        Kiss then, and lips that cannot speak ;
Blessing by silent vow :
Love, bless me ere I go.


When fragrant zephyrs blow,
        Some day,
        Sadly ;
Sighing a requiem soft and low,
        Some day ;
Swaying the leaves so mournfully and slow ;
        There I shall seem     ·
        To rise before you, as in a dream,
Over the spot where weeping willows bow,
And where sweet wild flowers grow.


When fading sunset's glow,
        Some day,
        Redly,
Casteth a parting gleam ere sinking low ;
        Some day,

Above my grave, bending in silent woe,
    Or kneeling there,
    Breathing a silent prayer,
To that low mound come thou,
Sobbing, " I loved her so !"


Yes, some day soon, though when I may not know ;
    Some day,
    Sadly,
When I lie sleeping the green sod below ;
    Some day
Thy anguished tears shall flow ;
    When I have passed away,
    Shall memory touch thy heart some day,
And thou wilt say,—oh ! why not tell me now ?—
" Dear one, I love thee *so !*"

THE END.

15